CW00358225

A CANDLELIGHT ROMANCE

35 p

BOOKCHOICE
EXCHANGEABLE
AT
HALF PRICE

CANDLELIGHT ROMANCES

BALI BREEZES

ESTHER BOYD

A CANDLELIGHT ROMANCE

Published by
Dell Publishing Co., Inc.
1 Dag Hammarskjold Plaza
New York, New York 10017

Copyright © 1980 by E.A.D. Boyd

All rights reserved. No part of this book may be repro-
duced or transmitted in any form or by any means,
electronic or mechanical, including photocopying, re-
cording or by any information storage and retrieval
system, without the written permission of the Publisher,
except where permitted by law.

Dell ® TM 681510, Dell Publishing Co., Inc.

ISBN: 0-440-10404-1

Printed in the United States of America
First printing—December 1980

CHAPTER ONE

"If you work at the hotel, surely you could smuggle me in to watch the *kecak* dance tonight." Claudia turned on her most scintillating smile for the benefit of the only other passenger in the open-sided native *boomibus,* a dark-skinned youth sitting on the wooden bench opposite.

"I am sorry, *nyonya* . . ." he began, flattering her by addressing her as "lady." There was something so appealing about the fair-haired American girl who had asked him if he was going to the Bali Breezes Hotel that he hesitated to give her an outright refusal of assistance.

"Oh, please!" she begged, her head cocked to the side and one forefinger pressed to her chin in a childlike gesture of supplication. "I can't leave Bali without seeing the *kecak* dance—it's the whole reason for my coming here, and the hotel is my only chance. If I could possibly afford the twenty-five dollars, I would pay for the buffet dinner and performance just like any other tourist. But I just don't have the money."

From appearance alone, the boy had every justification for doubting her poverty. Her pretty cotton dress and leather sandals, her fashionable denim shoulder bag, the makeup that accentuated her wide-set, gold-flecked eyes and generous mouth—all this suggested a guest at the hotel with plenty of cash to spend. Yet, what guest ever traveled in a *boomi*—only fifty cents to go half across the island—instead of in a taxi or a tourist bus?

"Well, it could be done, *nyonya*," he said, still dubious, "but you would have to watch from the side of the stage."

"I don't mind that," Claudia reassured him, "just as long as I have a good view of the dance. Tell me how to get in."

A few minutes later they were standing together at the foot of the two huge brick pillars, decorated with grinning stone gargoyles, which marked the main entrance to the famous oriental hotel. A smooth Tarmac drive curved away through a dense grove of palms and shrubbery toward the unseen fortress of the hotel. The tropical evening air seemed even more oppressive than usual; looking up, Claudia saw black storm clouds gathering overhead. Darkness was falling quickly.

"We will go this way." Her companion headed down a rough track that led away from the drive, plunging into the shadowy undergrowth. "This path leads to the staff quarters. I am going there to change into my uniform. You will take a turning to the right, and that will lead you to the back of the hotel. The first door you come to is the one that opens onto the back of the stage. It is kept locked until just before each performance, but I will be there in fifteen minutes to open it for you. Don't worry, *nyonya*, you will enjoy as good a view of the show as any of the paying customers."

Claudia caught a glimpse of flashing white teeth in the dim twilight. "That's terrific. You've really been very kind. I do have ten dollars . . ." She fumbled half-heartedly in her bag.

"No, you do not have to give me anything. Here is your turning. I will see you at the door in fifteen minutes."

The young waiter's silent shape vanished after a few footsteps, and Claudia started quickly down the way he had told her to go, anxious to reach her secret entrance before daylight faded altogether. At first the narrow path seemed as unreal as a dream. She felt herself breathing rapidly, scared yet determined, as she groped along its tortuous route. Once she let out a small cry as a leafy tendril brushed against her cheek. But she hurried on, scarcely aware of the damage being done to her hair and dress each time she veered off into the bushes on either side.

Suddenly she was in open ground. The sky, although still heavily overcast, afforded enough light for her to clearly see the outlines of hangarlike buildings that must be garages, and then, further on, other outhouses that must be annexes. Following instructions, she started moving along the wall of the multi-story hotel toward the sea. The murmur of breakers not far away restored her confidence that she was on the right track. The first door she came to would be the one.

Soon the light from lamp standards around the swimming pool became visible in the distance and illuminated Claudia's surroundings more clearly. She was walking along a grassy track between the wall and a thick hedge, and as she walked she felt the first heavy raindrops plop onto her head. All at once the still, sultry night was shattered by the violence of a gale-force wind; palm fronds waved wildly above her, and enormous drops of water beat against her body, soaking it within seconds. There was no protection from the lashing of the tropical storm until she came to the door she was seeking. As she expected, it was locked, but since it was recessed a foot or so into the wall, she could keep out of the direct blast of the wind and rain by flattening herself against it.

Only five minutes had passed since she had parted from her friend from the *boomi;* she gritted her teeth, resolved to stick it out for another ten. A live performance of the *kecak* dance was worth a good deal of discomfort.

She had reckoned her waiting time was nearly over when she saw a tall figure jogging toward her, his umbrella held sideways against the driving rain. He was coming in the same direction as she had, and within moments he would catch up with her. He had to pass right by her door; there was no hope of not being seen. Panic seized her. He was probably a guard patrolling the grounds. Her only chance was to nip out toward the swimming pool and then creep back to the door as soon as the man had gone. She ran out from the doorway onto the soggy grass and fled as fast as her flapping wet skirt would allow.

A deep-throated shout behind her told her that she had been too slow. Heavy footsteps slapping closer and closer confirmed that her pursuer was gaining on her. When her arm was roughly grabbed from behind, she knew that she had lost, and stopped running.

By now they had reached a point where the light was much better. She looked up resignedly into the face of her captor. He was in his twenties, good-looking in a classical way with curly fair hair, a square jaw, and a sturdy muscular build. In a striped T-shirt and white shorts he didn't look at all like a guard. Claudia immediately hoped that he might be a hotel guest who would have no right to detain her; her best approach might be to feign annoyance at being molested.

"Let go of my arm! What do you think you're doing?" she said angrily.

8

A broad grin replaced the man's initial look of surprise. He relaxed his grip, but still held her firmly. *"Fräulein!"* he exclaimed in an accent identical to that of her own German-émigré parents. "This is not the weather for the garden. You must have become yourself lost. Forgive me, for a thief I mistook you. Now I will escort you back to the hotel."

Claudia allowed herself to be led along, protected by the man's umbrella, to the swimming pool and then around the corner to the main entrance. As soon as she could, she would excuse herself from him and slip outside again back to the stage door.

He chatted amiably as they squelched their way across the grass. "You have been here some days? It is surprising that I have not before noticed you. You have been hiding yourself, *Fräulein.*"

"Not really." Claudia gave a noncommittal little laugh.

"It must be remedied immediately," the man went on, brimming with enthusiasm. "Tonight, for example, we have arranged a special performance of the *kecak* dance—in English the monkey dance is its name—with the best dancers in Bali. It is something you should not miss."

"I know," she said. "I intend to see it."

"Excellent! Permit me to introduce myself. Anton Reinholtz. I am the recreational director for the hotel. It is my responsibility to arrange the best possible sports and entertainment for our guests—swimming galas, golf, tennis, barbecue suppers, dance performances, anything that will please them."

"It must be an interesting job."

"It is. The manager, Mr. Fox, he is very strict for those who work for him, but to me he gives quite the free hand. I have new ideas in my mind also. If they are successful, and Mr. Fox's uncle hears about them,

9

then I hope I may obtain the promotion to one of the more important hotels in his international chain—Jamaica, perhaps, or Hawaii. Even better, one of the resort hotels in Europe. Ah, yes, I would be very happy to return to Europe. You knew of course, *Fräulein*, that the manager's uncle is Mr. Wilbur Fox, the president of Malibu Hotels Limited?"

"Er, no, I didn't actually," said Claudia vaguely.

"Oh, yes, indeed! He is as famous as Conrad Hilton himself. He lives in San Francisco, but fortunately for me, he spends much time here at Bali Breezes. He likes very much the chief dancer you will see tonight. And so it is good for me that I introduced her to our dance team. Herr Wilbur Fox remembers such things; it will help with my promotion. Yes, Negara was for me a lucky find."

His mention of the chief dancer pricked Claudia's interest. "Is this Negara a very good dancer?" she asked.

Anton shrugged. "Frankly, I do not know. I hired her on the advice of a friend. I am not an expert in the dance. Swimming, tennis, skiing—those I am expert in. I used to be skiing instructor in Germany."

I can see you wowing the girls on the slopes, thought Claudia, glancing sideways at his handsome Nordic features.

"You ski in Australia, *Fräulein?*" he went on. "You are with the Australian group, are you not—the one that arrived last week? Although you do not hit me as an Australian girl. Mostly they are tall and wide. But you are slender, delicate, and perhaps a little timid. You have many dates in Australia, *Fräulein?* Or someone special in your tour group perhaps?"

"I'm not Australian," said Claudia, "and I have no special boyfriend." She was on the point of adding that she wasn't even staying in the hotel, but checked herself in time. The best way of giving Anton Reinholtz the slip would be to pretend to be going to her room to change out of her wet clothes. They were just approaching the imposing entrance to the hotel. A doorman presided there, magnificently arrayed in the costume of a Balinese prince, with a double skirt and sash, a tight embroidered waistcoat, and a gold three-cornered crown. He stood back as a pair of huge plate-glass doors automatically slid open for them, grinning knowingly at Anton as they passed through.

"Well, thank you very much," said Claudia, stopping to face Anton as soon as they were in the lobby. "I must go and get out of these wet clothes now."

"Yes, it is important," he agreed. "Come, I will take you to the desk to fetch the key to your room."

"There's really no need . . ." she said, a touch of desperation in her voice.

"But of course. I am going to the desk myself." His hand closed around her arm again and he propelled her across the broad expanse of the lobby toward the desk.

Alarm overtook Claudia at once. How could she ask for a key when she didn't have a room?

"The lady would like her key," said Anton pleasantly. "What is your room number, *Fräulein*?"

Frantically Claudia scanned the long board hanging with keys. "Six-two-five," she said at random.

"Six-two-five?" echoed the clerk. "I think you must be mistaken, miss. Six-two-five is Dr. Williamson's room—it has been for over a year now. What is your name, please? I will be glad to look up your room number."

"It . . . it doesn't matter," she mumbled, turning away. "I . . . I'll just wait over there for my friend. I remember now; she took the key with her." She made a final effort to shake off Anton. "I'll be fine now, thanks." But she knew the effort was futile. She would have to come clean.

Claudia walked away from the desk and sat on one of the circular divans that furnished the lobby. Predictably, Anton perched beside her.

"Your room, *Fräulein* . . . I do not understand."

"I have no room, Mr. Reinholtz." She looked squarely into his innocent blue eyes. "I am not a guest in this hotel."

"But then, what were you doing in the garden in the rain? Who are you and why are you here?"

That would be a long story, thought Claudia, and not one she wanted to tell to a complete stranger. She could not expect Anton to understand, any more than her German parents had understood—why, after five years' steady work at the Philadelphia Insurance Company office and about due for promotion, she had given it all up to join a struggling semiprofessional modern dance group that barely paid her enough to keep alive. But then no one could appreciate how much she had hated the monotonous daily office routine.

The last straw for her honest but unimaginative parents had come a month ago when she had announced she was taking all her savings out of the bank to pay for this trip to Bali. Even her fellow dancers had thought she was slightly crazy. But after seeing a documentary film on Balinese dancing, it had struck her like a bolt of lightning that this was the most exciting thing she had ever come across.

For weeks afterward, she was haunted by the graceful movements of the dancers and the intricacy of their costumes. Determination gripped her; she too would learn to dance like that. There was only one way to learn—by going to Bali herself and studying the dancing first hand.

She had found a cheap excursion flight that allowed

her a full month on the island, but three weeks of it had already passed. In the village dancing schools she had learned a great deal, absorbing by dogged concentration much of the technique, but sadly she had come to realize that she could never dance as beautifully as the native Balinese girls.

Yet, she would go home in ten days' time with her ambition fulfilled, with her thirst for the Balinese people's unique form of expression assuaged, and with the knowledge that there probably wasn't another girl in the whole United States who had had the same training.

She had no intention of explaining all this to the powerfully built German who squatted beside her. "I'm a dancer," she said, "and I came to see the performance tonight. I . . . I got lost looking for the entrance."

"It is also very wet you got," said Anton, looking at her sopping dress and the wisps hanging from what had been a neat topknot of hair. "You will be sick from the pneumonia if you spend the evening in that dress. In here it is not like the outside, you know. We keep the temperature very cool all through the hotel; we find the guests prefer it. But that problem can be undone. You can buy a new dress at the little boutique over there." He pointed across the lobby to a row of small shops.

"Thank you for being concerned about me," she replied, "but I will be quite all right. Anyway I don't have enough money with me for a new dress. Please just leave me now. I'm sure you have things to do."

But Anton was not going to be shaken off so easily. He looked earnestly into her face, studying the freckles on her tilted nose and the amber-flecked eyes that so nearly matched her honey-blond hair. "How much money do you have, *Fräulein*? But I cannot ask you such a question while I continue to call you so impersonal. Tell it to me please, what is your name?"

"My name's Claudia. Claudia Bauer. And I have ten dollars."

"Ten dollars only! But it will cost you twenty-five dollars for the buffet and dance. You will not be able to go, you see?"

She leaped at the chance Anton's remark gave her. Getting up quickly, she said, "Is that so? Well, I'll just have to go home again, won't I?" She started toward the plate-glass doorway. "Thank you very much. Good night."

"No, no, no!" He had bounded after her and grabbed her arm again. "Where is it you live?"

"In Kuta, near the beach on the other side of the island. I . . . I have very little money, so I am staying in a guesthouse there." She revealed her financial situation deliberately; with this kind of glorified beach-boy, it was probably the quickest way to get rid of him.

"*Mein Gott!*" He smacked his forehead with his palm. "A girl like you is not safe in those places. They are full of hippies. Listen, Claudia! I have the solution for this evening. You will take your ten dollars and you will go over there and buy a dress with it. You can get a simple batik for that amount. Then I will meet you here in twenty minutes, and I will take you to the buffet and dance show."

Claudia had no intention of becoming obligated to this stranger, good-looking though he was. "I'm sorry, I couldn't do that. But thank you all the same."

"You do not understand. It is not I who pays for it. It is my privilege as the director to entertain people from outside the hotel. You will enjoy the excellent buffet and drinks as well—food such as you don't receive at your—ach!—guesthouse. You will see the

14

dance you came so far to see. And you will have a good dry dress to spend the evening in. So! It is settled?"

For the first time Claudia hesitated. It *was* a perfect solution to her dilemma. She could see the dance without really being beholden to Anton. She would get a good dinner instead of forgoing her meal altogether, as she had intended. And she would be comfortable instead of shivering in her present clammy clothes.

"Well . . ." she said, just before an uncontrollable sneeze burst from her, almost doubling her over with its intensity.

"*Liebchen!*" he cried. "Already you are beginning to freeze! Now you do it as I say. I must go for the short time; some important guests are expected to arrive in a few minutes. After that I will meet with you —right at this spot."

Claudia objected strongly to being called *Liebchen* by a man she hardly knew. It was a German term of endearment not to be used lightly, although Anton probably used it freely, and with success, on the girls he met in the hotel. But she still could not refuse his offer without forfeiting her opportunity to see the best performance in Bali of the famous monkey dance. She decided she could swallow a few *Liebchens* for the sake of the quest that had brought her to this far-off island in the Republic of Indonesia.

She stood erect, intending to accept his invitation graciously but rather haughtily. Unfortunately her teeth began to chatter as soon as she opened her mouth to speak. "Th . . . thank you, M . . . Mister Reinholtz. I w-will be pleased to m-meet you later."

He laughed, a gay, infectious laugh that the girls on the ski slopes must have loved, and laid a hand intimately on her shoulder. "Then go and change before your head falls off. It will be a pleasant evening, I

15

promise you. *Auf später!*" He was gone, striding purposefully toward the elevators.

While waiting for an elevator to arrive, he looked back at her, smiling. She gave him a little wave and headed off in the direction of the boutique with a jaunty step. The evening might yet be fun.

Ten minutes later she was back on the divan in the lobby. She wore a new simple, two-color batik sundress that had been marked at twelve dollars but cheerfully sold to her for ten. Her sandals, scrubbed clean in the ladies' room, gave the dress a casual, resort style that seemed appropriate. She had also reapplied her make-up, dried her hair under the automatic hand drier, and styled it loosely down her back instead of tying it up into a topknot. Anton had been kind to her and deserved the best she could make of herself under the circumstances.

Claudia felt good, no longer shivering but cool, comfortable, and eager to see the world-famous dance.

While waiting in the lobby, she became aware that an event of some importance was about to take place at the front entrance. A dozen bellhops were being marshaled into line by the bell captain. The assistant manager, a dapper little Balinese in a dark suit, had left his desk and was nervously checking the arrangement of furniture and flowers. An ensemble of six musicians squatted on a mat just inside the sliding doors, awaiting the signal to start playing their native flutes and drums.

Then from the elevator slowly stalked a figure who instantly caught Claudia's attention. Dressed in immaculate pin-striped pants, black alpaca jacket, and white shirt with dark tie, his lanky frame towered over the short Balinese around him. He even stood head and shoulders above the motley group of rather sloppily dressed tourists who had gathered expectantly in groups around the lobby, wondering what all the fuss was about.

The man was in his early thirties, Claudia guessed, and had a somewhat vague, scholastic air about him, like the professor at an ivy-covered university. He wore heavy-rimmed glasses on his aquiline nose, and a lock of straight dark-brown hair strayed constantly across his forehead, to be swept back absently from time to time as he made his way across the thick pile carpet of the lobby. His cheeks were sallow, almost gaunt, as though he seldom ventured into the tropical sunshine, and his thin-lipped mouth was set into a severe, uncompromising line.

On the man's appearance from the elevator, the hotel staff instinctively drew to attention. The assistant manager bustled up to him to say something that was acknowledged with a curt nod, then followed him meekly to the entrance.

Through the hotel entrance doors, Claudia saw two long black limousines draw up. The magnificently attired doorman opened the doors of the first one with a flourish and a bow. Three Arabs in white robes stepped out in labored succession, their headdresses held in place by the ornamental gold bands that signified their status as highly placed sheikhs. Two were quite old; the third, in dark glasses, was younger.

While the Arabs were walking from their car toward the entrance, the lean, commanding figure in the black alpaca jacket positioned himself just inside and waited impassively. Claudia noticed that Anton had reappeared and had taken his place beside the assistant manager, two paces behind and to the right. Having changed out of the white shorts he had been wearing, he now was dressed in a pair of pale blue pants, neatly creased, and a plain white T-shirt that stretched tightly across his broad chest; the short sleeves were almost

17

bursting under the strain of his massive biceps. He looked every inch the sports-minded athletic instructor he was—a remarkable contrast to the much taller, slimmer, dark-suited man in front of him.

It was clear to Claudia by now that this must be Huntley Fox, the hotel manager whom Anton had mentioned with a certain reverence. Now that she had seen him, Claudia wasn't in the least surprised that he had a reputation for strictness.

The doors slid open under the command of their magic eye, and the Arabs filed slowly into the lobby. Huntley Fox stepped forward and shook the hand of each one with serious ceremony. Anton moved forward too in the hope of being introduced, but the manager merely indicated both him and the assistant manager with a casual wave of his hand. He then led the honored visitors across the lobby, nodding thoughtfully at the younger one with dark glasses who was speaking to him, his dour expression unchanged.

Eventually the four men disappeared into an elevator. A team of bellhops now carried in mountains of luggage, as the second limousine was unloaded under the direction of the bell captain. The musicians ceased the querulous tune of welcome that they had begun as soon as the Arabs had appeared, and started packing up their instruments. Tourists wandered aimlessly through the lobby again, resuming a general murmur of conversation, and with the manager gone, the staff, too, relaxed.

Claudia spotted Anton coming over to meet her, and rose with a smile as he approached. She couldn't help wondering what was going on upstairs—how the strange, unyielding character of Huntley Fox was coping with what must be equally insistent, and probably unusual, requests from the three powerful sheikhs who were temporarily committed to

18

his care. It must take a strong, decisive person, Claudia thought, to be the manager of a large, expensive hotel.

"No longer the poor little drowned mouse!" Anton beamed at her when he reached her side. "Such a pretty dress you have chosen! And your hair—far more enchanting than tied into a knob like a ballerina."

"But I am a ballerina—of sorts," she replied. "It's true, Anton; I only came to your hotel because I have to see the *kecak* dance. And I only came to Bali because I want to study Balinese dancing."

"You are a ballet dancer?" he said. "With some famous ballet company? You dance with Rudolf Nureyev perhaps? Certainly you have the grace." He stood back and looked her up and down as though she were a racehorse. "And the figure."

"You're jumping to conclusions again," Claudia smiled. "I'm not a ballet dancer in the classical sense. But I am a student of other traditional and modern forms of dancing, and I practice it myself with a group in Philadelphia. I find it less restrictive than classical ballet."

"And gymnastics? I am myself a gymnast."

"I've done some gymnastics—it's good exercise for loosening you up, but there's no freedom of expression in gym."

Anton shook his curly head in incomprehension, but his eyes were smiling as he took her arm. "Come, it is the time to go to eat. And after the food, we will watch the monkey dance together, and you can tell me more about freedom of expression. I think I like that—the freedom of expression. I may allow myself a little of that freedom before the evening is finish." He gave her elbow a quick, hard squeeze, and Claudia wondered anew whether she had been wise to accept his invitation. Gallant though he tried to be, he really wasn't her kind of man.

CHAPTER TWO

The evening's festivities were to be held in a large, high-ceilinged room used by the hotel for conventions and banquets. A stage was recessed into one wall. Tables and chairs were arranged in two rows along the other three sides, except for one section where a buffet table and bar had been set up. When Anton guided Claudia into the room, several parties of diners were already hungrily devouring their meal, and a queue at the buffet moved slowly down it.

"You and I will occupy this table," said Anton, leading the way to a small table adjacent to the large open space in front of the stage. Claudia noticed that it was next to one with a "reserved" sign on it, and would give them a ringside view of the dance. She was glad now that she was out front instead of hidden in the wings. Back there she would have seen only half the performance. Fate had, after all, smiled on her tonight.

The sight of the food made Claudia's mouth water. Delighted to have a change from her landlady's eternal rice dishes, she chose beef *satay*—thin wooden skewers holding small pieces of steak dipped in peanut-flavored sauce—and *bakmi goreng*, appetizing egg noodles mixed with grilled lobster tail and thinly sliced cucumber.

Anton took two ladles of *sambal*, a spicy-sauce thick

with liver and vegetables, saying that it was reputed to endow the consumer with strength and vitality, and a large piece of filet mignon in addition to smaller amounts of other dishes. His plate was almost overflowing as they proceeded to their table.

"You are content with the selection?" he asked her unnecessarily as they sat down. She assured him that it looked like the most delicious dinner she had ever eaten. He grinned at her with satisfaction and ceased his usual steady flow of conversation until he had cleaned his plate. Then he invited her to join him for a second serving, and when she declined, he excused himself and went back to the queue, leaving Claudia to sip the cup of black Java coffee that a waiter had brought her.

Her hunger pleasantly assuaged, Claudia looked around the room. Nearly all the tables were taken by now, except the reserved one next to her; there were laughing groups of Australians, washing down their food with beer; a party of Japanese taking turns photographing each other; and numbers of other tourists, many of them red-skinned, middle-aged and overweight, all enjoying themselves immensely. This was a very different type of audience from the small, aesthetic group that attended her performances in Philadelphia.

She watched Anton leave the buffet with another steaming plateful and start making his way toward her, but he was waylaid en route. Three tall, well-built girls with bare, deeply tanned shoulders and backs caught him as he passed their table and tried to persuade him to join them. One of them jumped up and kissed him on the cheek; they giggled as another pulled at his T-shirt. Claudia had ample proof of his popularity with the opposite sex, and a warm, slightly smug feeling crept over her when she saw him extricate himself from their grasp and nod in her direction to indicate that he already had a partner for the evening.

Three pairs of jealous eyes turned toward her. Then the girl who had kissed him threw back her hair and laughed, giving him a friendly pat on the bottom to send him on his way. Claudia looked in the other direction, blushing at the girl's blatant implication. Not only was Anton popular—he obviously enjoyed a certain reputation as well. She hoped she could end the evening without any problems.

"I seem to be unfairly monopolizing you," she said as he sat down beside her. "Don't you have a duty to be sociable with your tennis pupils or whoever those girls are?"

"Ach! Those are three Australians. They are nothing to me, although one of them is an Olympic swimmer. Very fast."

"You can say *that* again," murmured Claudia.

"I promise you, *Liebchen*, you interest me more than all three of them thrown together," he said between mouthfuls.

"Anton," she said, "before we go any further, I wish you wouldn't call me that . . . that name. Remember, I hardly know you."

He stopped eating and looked at her in surprise, trying to determine whether the serious tone in her voice was genuine. "What is so wrong with that? I like you—that is enough, is it not? Besides, you probably do not know what means the word."

"Of course I do!" she replied tartly. "It's absurd for you to call me your little love, your darling. Other girls might not mind, but I do. It's what my father used to call me, and sometimes still does. And I love my father very much."

"Your father?" echoed Anton, his blue eyes wide

with astonishment. "Your father speaks German? I thought you came from America."

"I do, but I was born in Germany, and went to Pennsylvania with my parents when I was three years old. That was twenty years ago, but we often speak German at home. My mother's English still isn't very good and I'm fluent in German."

"It is true what you say? I know that in parts of Canada one speaks the French tongue, but German in America . . . ? What part of Germany do you come from?"

"The northwest. Near Hanover."

"It is a miracle!" exclaimed Anton. "I too am from Hanover. Now I know what I so instantly saw when I found you in the rain. You remind me of the girls I used to know when I was at home. Claudia, we are like brother and sister!" He laid a heavy hand on hers.

"Then let it stay that way," she retorted, drawing her hand away quickly and hiding it under the table. "Brothers and sisters don't usually hold hands."

A brief cloud of annoyance passed across Anton's brow; then he laughed uneasily and continued eating. When he had finished, he wiped his mouth carefully and cupped his chin in his hand, gazing intently into her eyes.

"I am sorry," he said contritely. "With you I see that I must move more slowly. It was the same with the . . . the old-fashioned girls back home. You will forgive me, Claudia?"

She couldn't help smiling at his candor. "Yes, I'll forgive you," she said. "But I must warn you, Anton. With me it would be better if you didn't move at all."

He didn't answer that, but instead suggested that they share a bottle of chilled German Moselle wine to celebrate their kindred spirits. Claudia hadn't the heart to refuse the celebration; besides, a glass of dry

Moselle would taste good after the sticky rice wine that was all she was able to afford in Kuta when she had a drink with friends there. This evening was certainly a far cry from the frugality of her life during the nearly three weeks she had been in Bali. She hadn't realized until now how much she missed life's small luxuries. It would be hard to go back to the boarding-house.

The waiter cleared away their plates and brought the wine in an ice bucket. Anton insisted on clinking glasses with her in the European gesture of flirtation. They had just taken their first sip when Claudia became aware of a hush settling across the room. The waiter beside them stiffened perceptibly. Anton himself drew back from her and sat upright in his chair.

Half turning to see what had caused this sudden change in atmosphere, Claudia observed a small procession moving from the door toward the reserved table beside them. First came the headwaiter, straight as a ramrod; behind him came the three Arab sheikhs in single file, the two with gray beards and watery eyes leading, and the younger one, still wearing his dark glasses, behind them. Bringing up the rear was Huntley Fox, his long legs loping along like a stealthy panther picking his way silently through the jungle. His features were as impassive as before, but as he drew closer, Claudia could see lines of weariness around his mouth, extending toward his firm jaw. Behind his glasses, dark eyelashes blinked as though they were longing to close. The manager seemed to be exerting a tremendous effort to maintain his dignity and concentration in a state close to exhaustion. Seldom had she seen such a display of tight self-discipline.

The headwaiter seated the foursome with elaborate courtesy, Huntley Fox next to the Arab in dark glasses.

It appeared that he spoke English and acted as interpreter for the other two. When they were settled, the buzz of conversation broke out again. The manager disdainfully surveyed the room, catching Anton's eye as he did so. Anton nodded and smiled a greeting at him, receiving a flicker of recognition in return. Then Huntley Fox turned his full attention to his Arab guests, and Anton relaxed.

"The dance will soon to begin," Anton said to Claudia. "You will be pleased for that, I know."

"You're right," she said. "I can't wait. I've been practicing the Balinese style by watching movies, but the only way to learn is to watch the real thing. I'm longing to see the girl who dances the *Sayang* go into her trance. I suppose that part will be played by your chief dancer, Negara."

"You know about the monkey dance already? I thought you had come to see . . ." asked Anton, with a puzzled frown.

"I've never seen it done live before, but, as I told you, I've been studying the Balinese dances and their folklore for some time. This will probably be the version with Rama, the exiled prince, and Sita, his wife, in the monkey forest after she has been kidnapped by the demon king."

"Claudia! Claudia, I have it!" Anton suddenly cried, excitement showing all over his face. "All evening I have been thinking . . . trying to find some way . . . and now I have it."

"What do you have, Anton? I don't understand."

"A way you can be rescued from those hippies in Kuta and come to Bali Breezes. You can come here to work! One of the new ideas I have for the guests is a class for exercises, the gymnastics for keeping the body fit. But he,"—Anton motioned toward the manager at the next table—"he always say the guests not will be interested, that they can get keep-fit classes at wherever they come from."

"I'm sure he's right. Every town has a health club these days. In the United States anyway."

"Perhaps." Anton shrugged, still bubbling with enthusiasm. "But don't you see? If we were to offer a course in Balinese dancing, that would be something unique, something they could not get at their home. And you could teach the class! In English, German, and French! He will surely agree to that. And you will be under my department!"

"It's a nice idea," said Claudia. "I could certainly do it, and I think I could make it interesting too, though I'm not sure my French is up to it. I'd like to stay longer. And my earnings would pay my extra air fare home."

"I will ask if we can see him after the dance. Heaven has sent me this inspiration! You will agree, Claudia?"

"All right," said Claudia. "If you think he'd take me on." The idea certainly had merit. She could teach and learn at the same time, and it would postpone the day, now close at hand, when her funds ran out altogether and she had to go home, still only half knowing about the fabulous Balinese culture that had continued for over a thousand years. The only problem would be Anton himself. He seemed a persistent character. But she could keep him at arm's length, she reckoned, until he got tired of her and started chasing some other girl. Yes, she decided, it was a good idea. She stole a glance at the stony-faced manager a few feet away. He didn't look the type to be in the least interested in such cultural activities. Or did he? Underneath his fierce pose as a disciplinarian, he did have an intellectual, professorial air about him. Perhaps Anton could persuade him.

Anton licked his lips and rose from his chair. The occupants of the next table were sitting in silence, staring at the empty stage in front of them. Behind them the tourists were getting noisier as the liquor flowed more freely, and Huntley Fox's brow was now settled into a permanent frown. Anyone could see that this wasn't the best moment to approach the boss with a request, but there was no stopping Anton now.

Huntley Fox had noticed him get up, and didn't move his head when Anton spoke to him from behind. Neither did his expression change; he glanced briefly at Claudia, who forced a shy smile in return, and then looked back at the blank stage again, still totally inert. Finally he gave a brief nod, and his thin lips moved for a fraction of a second; Anton was dismissed.

"He'll see us in his office after the show," Anton whispered excitedly as he took his seat beside Claudia.

"He didn't look very keen on what you said to him, or on me either. I felt like sinking through the floor."

"Don't worry about that. Always he is the same. For the hotel he has no emotion—only business. But for Negara . . . that is another story. You will see."

Claudia didn't have a chance to ask what she would see, because at that moment two overhead spotlights came on, forming bright pools in front of the stage. Then the lights in the rest of the room were turned off, and a loudspeaker announced the beginning of the famous *kecak* dance. The tourist hubbub faded almost to silence. The spectacle that Claudia had struggled through a tropical rainstorm and against serious financial odds to witness was at last about to commence.

The *kecak* dance is performed entirely without musical accompaniment or stage props of any kind. Claudia gasped as a hundred dark-brown young men, clad only in black-and-white-checkered loin cloths, ran onto the bare floor a few feet from their table and formed themselves into a semicircle five or six deep, squatting cross-legged facing the stage. Both arms raised above their heads, they began swaying from side to side, rhythmically making a noise in unison that sounded like "Ch-ch-ch-ch." They kept this up for the whole dance, sometimes augmented by weird Eastern chanting from their leader, and varying the pitch of their noise to represent sympathy, excitement, or anger as the story indicated. Nothing could have more closely simulated a band of chattering monkeys as they watched the dramatic action taking place on the stage.

The first scene was the arrival of Rama and Sita, the prince and princess, lost in the forest. The prince was a smooth-skinned young man in an elaborate costume and a gold crown. He swayed and moved his head and arms with infinite grace, scarcely shifting his feet in accordance with the mode of Balinese dancing. His control was superb, his poise perfect for his role as a monarch.

The princess surprised her. Dressed equally regally in a strapless gold bodice and long green-and-white batik skirt, her bare skin was far paler than the prince's. This didn't appear to be makeup, for her feet—none of the dancers wore shoes—were equally pale. She was also several inches taller than the young man, a difference emphasized by the rather stiff erectness of her body; her hips and knees moved without much supple grace. However, her long, slender arms, decorated with silver bangles, were beautifully expressive, and she had totally mastered the difficult technique of stretching out her fingers and moving them sideways to touch the next one in rapid succession. In short, her artistry didn't seem to come as naturally to her as it did to her partner and to the girls Claudia had seen dancing informally in the villages; though skillful, it seemed more foreign and painfully acquired.

Her features too suggested a degree of European ancestry.

But if Claudia found imperfections—from the point of view of pure Balinese dancing—in her physique and ability, it was clearly apparent that Huntley Fox did not. Anton had nudged her and whispered, "That's Negara," as soon as the princess had entered the semi-circle of arm-swaying monkeys. It was purely by chance that, a moment or two later, Claudia's field of vision had wandered to include the manager. Huntley Fox's lassitude had vanished. He was leaning forward intently, his features taut and concentrated.

So! thought Claudia. It isn't only Wilbur Fox who is enamored of Negara. His nephew Huntley is equally smitten.

As the dance proceeded the manager took off his glasses from time to time, revealing heavy-lidded dark brown eyes. The weary blinking had gone, replaced by an intense gaze of adoration. He appeared to be completely entranced by Negara, oblivious of his Arab guests. If Huntley Fox had a weakness that could distract him from his rigid self-discipline as a hotel manager, that weakness was Negara.

When Rama, the prince, had been enticed from Negara's side by an accomplice of the demon king, she danced a duet with the demon's captive niece, herself a lovely girl, but not nearly as striking a beauty as Negara, nor as experienced a dancer. But the other girl's wide oriental eyes and the slow, sinuous movements of her hips were more genuinely Balinese, it seemed to Claudia.

Later, when a grotesque masked creature in white tights and gloves appeared and threatened the two girls, they both used their long crimson sashes to ward off their attacker and pointed two fingers at the evil one in self-protection. Claudia found herself able to believe in the other girl's ability to resist the wicked beast by means of these allegorical gestures, but Negara only appeared to be executing a complicated routine. She seemed as foreign to the nuances of Balinese dancing as Claudia would be herself.

True, from her greater height, Negara could swing her waist-length hair more defiantly—and, judging by the quivering of Huntley Fox's lower lip—more seductively than the other girl, but Claudia found her style disappointing. She wondered how much Negara owed her position as principal dancer to the strength of her personal appeal to the manager.

At last the dance drew to a close with the rescue of the princess by her husband and the slaying of the demon king. The monkeys' jubilation rose to a screeching crescendo; they lay down on their backs, clapping wildly in tune with the beat of their incessant "Ch-ch-ch." Negara flitted from the stage with a bow that acknowledged the audience's applause, but did not include her fellow performers. The monkeys' noise diminished to silence as they fled into the wings, and the bare floor, which for an hour had been the scene of strange, primitive activity, became suddenly empty.

Claudia looked at Huntley Fox. He was wiping his eyes and replacing his glasses, once more assuming his role as polite host. With a wan smile at the Arabs, he ushered them from the room. A buzz of talk and laughter immediately engulfed Claudia and Anton. The fact that all those tourists had been able to keep quiet throughout the dance was testimony to its attention-holding quality. Claudia herself felt uplifted and satisfied, although she had to admit to herself that it was the chorus of monkeys and the grace of the second-string performers that had fascinated her more than the skill of the principal dancer.

"So," exclaimed Anton, pushing back his chair, "now

you have seen the monkey dance. You are pleased with our performance?"

"Oh, yes, very pleased. Thank you for bringing me," replied Claudia sincerely.

"And Negara? She is beautiful, is she not? And a great dancer?"

"She's certainly beautiful," Claudia admitted, but added cautiously, "But I found her dancing rather . . . wooden, while the essential quality of Balinese dancing is its fluidity. Compared to the others, she seemed cold somehow, and not to have her heart in it."

Anton laughed. "Yes, the cold heart, that is Negara. You observe it well; you see it in her dancing also."

"Are you sure she's a hundred percent Balinese? She looks . . ."

"No," said Anton, "only a half. I found her in a nightclub in Jakarta. Her mother was from Bali; her father, who knows? A sailor, it is thought, perhaps Portuguese."

"She does look partly European."

"But that is the big advantage for her. Girls with mixed blood—they are often the most beautiful, no?"

"To some people perhaps, men especially. But there's something about the way the Balinese dance that no other race can copy. I know I could never do it myself if I tried forever."

"But you agree that she is beautiful?" Anton persisted. Claudia remembered that he had a good deal at stake in the fact of Negara's beauty.

"Oh, yes. And the manager thinks so too; that's for sure. She almost had him hypnotized."

"Always he watches her like that. I think it is the only time he forget his work. That and when he flies his helicopter."

"He flies a helicopter? It's funny, I wouldn't have thought that . . ." Somehow she couldn't imagine the tall, stern-looking Huntley Fox at the controls of a helicopter. She had always thought of pilots as more carefree, daredevil types. But then she had never even met the man, and looks could be deceiving. Unless she had seen it with her own eyes, she wouldn't have thought him capable of being so captivated by a little dancer either. There must be more to Huntley Fox than was apparent at first glance, she decided.

"Come, Claudia!" Anton interrupted her musing. "Let us not waste the time talking about him. We will go and see him now. We will tell him about your new job."

"I haven't got it yet, Anton," she said. "It was only your idea, you know. And he didn't seem very impressed when you mentioned it to him before the dance."

"Pah!" replied Anton, dismissing her doubt with a casual wave. "He was thinking of Negara, that was all. Never be fearful; he will see that my idea is good. But he is not one who likes to wait for the appointment. We must go at once to his office."

Anton took Claudia's hand to lead her from the room, which was still full of tourists, drinking and laughing and imitating the dancers they had just watched. The three Australian girls waved and nudged each other as they came near. Claudia quickly removed her hand from Anton's grasp.

The hotel management offices were on the second floor, facing inland. Despite their poor location, they were very comfortably appointed around a large open area for clerks and typists. Anton proudly pointed out his own office, a small one in a remote corner. Claudia sensed that he wasn't quite as high up the ladder as he would have her believe.

This impression was heightened when Anton knocked reverently on a large wooden door at the far end of the typist's area. To reach it they had passed through an empty cubicle used by the hotel manager's secretary to insulate him from visitors. A deep voice from inside called to them to enter, and Anton opened the door to let Claudia pass through first.

The office was immense, part of a suite that included an anteroom and a bedroom. Easy chairs were grouped around several coffee tables, the walls covered with Japanese bark cloth, scattered with interesting modern paintings. The decor was in excellent taste, worthy of the cosmic empire that was run from the desk on the far side, under the window. A familiar lanky figure sat there, his head bowed over papers.

Huntley Fox didn't look up from whatever he was writing as Claudia and Anton padded across the carpet to the solid, leather-topped desk. "Sit down," he said brusquely, and they each took one of the upright chairs facing the desk. While they waited for his attention, Claudia studied the gaunt, remorseless features of the manager as he concentrated on his work. The stray lock of hair drooped over one frame of his glasses, and his jaw was set square as if his memo were sealing someone's fate.

At last he laid down his pen and leaned back in his swivel chair, brushing back the lock of hair and taking off his glasses. The eyes, which quickly flicked from one to the other of his visitors, held none of the fire that they had poured onto Negara, but they were dark and piercing nevertheless. Claudia felt herself wilt under their scrutiny.

"Well, Anton," said the manager, stifling a yawn, "what is it you want again?" His voice had a slight Boston accent.

Anton leaned forward eagerly. "Huntley, I'd like you to meet Miss Claudia Bauer. I think she could be very useful to us."

The manager stared at Claudia more critically now. She felt him summing her up. "Do you spell that B-o-w-e-r?" he asked.

"No," she said, giving him the correct spelling.

"So you must be German," he said. "A friend of Anton's, I suppose. I must warn you, Anton, we don't have any use for patronage in this hotel."

"I'm not a friend of Anton's," said Claudia at once. "I mean . . . I only met him this afternoon."

"With Anton friendships develop quickly. Especially with attractive German girls." A ghost of a smile crossed Huntley Fox's face.

"I'm not German. I'm American, though my parents come from Germany."

"So you're probably from Cleveland, Ohio," stated the manager flatly, still fixing her with his penetrating gaze.

"Actually I'm not; I'm from Philadelphia, but how did you know there were a lot of people from the old country in Cleveland?"

"One of the pieces of useless knowledge I tend to pick up," he replied drily, making Claudia feel small and snubbed. "Well, what is it you think you can do for us, Miss Bauer?"

Anton cut in enthusiastically. "She's a student of oriental dance, Huntley—knows so very much about Balinese dancing. The perfect one to take the class in how to dance, which I suggest to you; the guests will be crazy for it. She speaks the three languages also— the English, the French, and the German."

"A pity she doesn't speak Arabic too," said Huntley Fox wearily. "That I could have used this evening."

Anton laughed politely. "The sheikhs do not wish to dance, only to observe," he said. "But I am sure that the ladies—the ones who are a little fat perhaps . . ."

"I've told you before, Anton," the manager said

testily. "We don't need a health club at Bali Breezes. This isn't a fitness camp."

"But my plan is not for the fitness only," Anton argued. "It is for culture. I know you interest yourself in that. The guests could learn the dances as well as watch them. See how they practice on their own after each monkey dance is over. Claudia—I mean Miss Bauer—could teach them the proper way."

"You know as well as I do that they're just playing the fool when they do that—full of liquor and corning off. You'd be lucky if you found enough guests to fill two classes a week, and we can't take on a whole new staff member just for that, especially a non-local. You know my policy is to employ Balinese wherever possible. Now, if I could persuade Negara to take a few classes in her spare time . . ." A wistful glaze came over Huntley Fox's eyes as he mentioned her name, but he quickly recovered himself. "I'm sorry, Anton, Miss Bauer, but I'm afraid it's out of the question."

Claudia started to rise from her chair, but Anton still refused to let the verdict stand. With what Claudia thought was fearful gall, he said to Huntley Fox, "But Negara does not like the teaching. Even your uncle, Herr Wilbur, cannot persuade her."

A dark cloud crossed the manager's face. "No," he said tartly. "Even my uncle cannot persuade her. By the way, he's coming here at the end of next week, Anton. Try and keep him busy on the golf course, will you. And find him some drinking companions if you can. I want him out of my hair during the day and in a stupor at night."

Anton smiled a mischievous smile. "I will try during the day, Huntley. But the night—that is his business, is it not? Anyway, I will try to make him happy, do not worry."

Huntley Fox returned the wry grin. "I know you

35

will, Anton. It's in your interest, and that is something you look after very well. I'm sorry I can't oblige you with regard to your relationship with Miss Bauer."

Anton opened innocent, wide eyes, "Miss Bauer? She is not . . ."

"Never mind," the manager cut in. "I'm sure she's not. But I'm not going to give you access to her as a member of your recreational department, and that's that."

Claudia had been half out of her chair all through this last exchange, and the manager's final insinuations made her get up completely, somewhat annoyed. Anton rose too and, with a curt good night, started for the door.

Claudia followed him across the wide expanse of the manager's office, and out of the door toward the elevators. Suddenly she heard the deep American voice calling, "Miss Bauer!"

She paused and turned round. Anton, who was a little ahead of her, turned back and stood with her at the office door. "Yes, Huntley," he said. "Did you want something?"

"Not you, Anton," barked the manager's voice. "It's Miss Bauer I want. Come back in here, Miss Bauer, and shut the door. I'd like to talk to you for a minute."

"I'll wait for you down the stairs," Anton hissed in anger, as Claudia moved slowly back into Huntley Fox's office, closing the door behind her.

CHAPTER THREE

Leaning back in his swivel chair, the tips of his fingers pressed together, Huntley Fox watched Claudia walk back to his desk. Why had he called her back? Why, particularly, had he called her back alone, without Anton? She was not normally afraid of people, but the lanky, spectacled man behind the desk filled her with a strange uneasiness bordering on fear.

Although her pulse was beating faster than usual, she managed to hide her apprehension and not to appear nervous as she sat down again opposite him. "Yes, Mr. Fox?" she inquired in a tone of surprised expectancy, demurely folding her hands in her lap.

"I have a proposition to put to you, Miss Bauer," he said. "It's your knowledge of the German language that prompted it—not your ability as a dancer, nor any physical attributes that you think you may possess."

"Oh." She couldn't think of anything more brilliant to say until he explained further.

"You have another asset that would be useful under the circumstances," he went on, staring at the ceiling now. "Can you think what that might be?"

"No." It was becoming increasingly difficult to maintain her composure in the presence of Huntley Fox. She began to wish the interview would come to an end as soon as possible. But some unknown force kept her riveted to her chair.

"Exactly what you are demonstrating now," he continued, taking off his glasses and fixing her with his dark, inscrutable eyes. "Patience to listen while others talk. A pleasant change from your friend Anton Reinholtz, for example."

"He's not really a friend . . ." she began, but he waved aside her protest.

"Your relationship with my recreational director is no concern of mine," he said dryly. "But I imagine that you are smart enough to recognize the kind of man he is, even after so short an acquaintance."

Claudia forced a smile but said nothing.

"Good," he said after a brief pause. "You don't answer. Most girls would have leaped to the defense of the person who had wined and dined them—and even bought them a new dress for the occasion."

She couldn't let this remark pass without comment, however much he wanted her to remain dumb. "I bought this dress myself," she said indignantly.

He raised his heavy eyebrows. "Did you now? In that case, my informant in the front lobby was wrong. I understood that you arrived in the hotel looking like a drowned rat, and that Anton had sent you to the boutique in the lobby to buy something clean and dry to wear. Also that you let your long fair hair down while you were changing—obviously with the intention of making yourself as attractive as possible for your benefactor."

"Mr. Fox," said Claudia, clipping her words, "I thought you said that my relationship with your recreational director was no concern of yours. Would you please tell me why you called me back into your office? I have a long way to go to get home tonight. My guest-house is away at Kuta Beach."

"Ah . . ." he nodded understandingly. "So you came over here just to watch the *kecak* dance? Did you bring with you the necessary twenty-five dollars?"

"No, I didn't. I couldn't possibly afford your scandalous prices." The courage that prompted Claudia to criticize the hotel to the face of its intimidating manager sparked, as it sometimes did under similar circumstances, an uncontrollable devilment—a metaphorical nose-thumbing to add spice to her brave words. "As a matter of fact, I had a plan all worked out to get in to see the show for nothing." Huntley Fox's astonished look made her smile—a dimple appeared in her cheek and her eyes sparkled with delight. "But unfortunately it didn't work out."

"I see." The manager's features composed themselves again into their usual nonchalance. "In that case, no wonder you were pleased to take advantage of Anton's generosity. Tell me, how do you intend to repay him for it when you leave here and meet him downstairs as he instructed you just now?"

"Mr. Fox!"

He held up a hand to silence her. "All right, I won't pursue that line any further. As you say, it's none of my business. We will talk instead of something that is. Miss Bauer, do your interests in Balinese culture extend any further than just the dancing? Do you know anything about their ancient art of wood-carving, for example?"

"A little. I know that there are four different grades, and that most of the pieces offered by hawkers on the street are very poor quality, mass-produced by unskilled peasants, while the good pieces of so-called professor's quality . . ."

"Very good." He sounded like a schoolmaster addressing an almost hopeless student who has for once given a correct answer. "And what do you know about the subject matter of the carvings?"

"Personally, I prefer the mythical subjects, the god Wismu, the fabulous bird Garuda, and so on. But some of the traditional designs are nice too. Why are you asking me all these questions, Mr. Fox?"

"One moment, Miss Bauer. I said just now that I thought you had patience; do you want me to change my mind?"

"No." The confession slipped out before she had considered what it implied. Why did she care about his opinion of her? Why was she submitting herself to this cross-examination anyway? She was letting herself be browbeaten by an insufferable, superior inquisitor. She couldn't think how she had let herself get into this position. "I mean I think I have a right to know what I'm doing here at this time of night in your office. You've already said you don't require my services."

"I haven't said that at all. All I said was that I cannot employ you as a dance instructor. Now, one more question. In spite of your personal preference, could you tolerate, even show approval, of someone who admired the long, thin surrealist type of carving that is also produced on this island? One of the guests, for instance."

"Oh, yes. Anybody is entitled to his own taste. But I don't approve of shoddy workmanship any more than I do of mediocre dancing." Although she was thinking of Negara as she said it, Claudia felt sure that Huntley Fox wouldn't catch the reference.

"I'm glad you said that. It's exactly the attitude I'm looking for." He leaned back in his chair, apparently relieved. She sensed that she had passed a test of some kind. Now perhaps the meaning of all this would be made clear. She waited expectantly.

"Your views on batik-making are presumably the same. Your choice of dress from the boutique downstairs demonstrates that. For the same price elsewhere —although I refuse to let them be sold in this hotel— you could have bought something in far more striking colors but made by an inferior process. I like your insistence on quality; I share your conviction entirely. What's more, I share your deep interest in the folklore and crafts of Bali. You won't find your friend Anton able to discuss these topics with you, you know. All he cares about is sport and women—and his personal ambitions, of course."

Claudia was unable to disagree with the manager's scathing summing-up of Anton's interests, although she resented the way he had been dragged into the conversation again. "Maybe he doesn't have time," she said weakly.

"Time?" Huntley Fox spat out the word. "He has all the time in the world. I'm the one who has no time. Yet since I've been here, I've learned a lot about the native people and am very much concerned with their welfare. I'm glad you are the same, because I'm about to offer you a job, Miss Bauer."

At last, she thought. He took long enough getting around to it. "And what would that be?" she asked. It would have to be a pretty good job if it meant working at all closely with *him*. She wouldn't be able to stand too much of this pedagogue approach.

"You'll be on a week's trial period," he said. "Next week will be an excellent opportunity to try you out. A small party of German industrialists is coming here with their wives. At the moment they're in Jakarta holding important trade talks with the Indonesian government; at the conclusion of the talks, the government is flying them to Bali for a holiday. The president of the country wants them to go back to Germany very impressed with what they've seen. It's been left to me to see that they are."

"But where do I come in?"

"One moment. The men, I am told, speak good English, but their wives don't speak it well, if at all. I will do my best to entertain the husbands, but I want you to take care of the wives. There will be three of them, all well-educated and involved women from the reports I've had. You will have to take them around, accompany them to the native dances, wood-carving and batik factories, and be able to answer—in German, of course—anything they want to know. These are not to be standard guided tours, you understand, but a personal introduction to Balinese culture taken by a qualified conductor. Do you think you're up to that?"

Claudia hesitated. "It depends. I would have to learn a lot more myself first, especially about the batik-making. And my knowledge of the history and folklore is pretty shaky."

"You have three days to acquaint yourself with all the detail you'll need—starting tomorrow. Your salary will begin then, and a room in the hotel and all meals will be provided. You will be a member of my personal staff, not in any way connected with the recreational director. And you will have to account to me if the visiting ladies aren't completely delighted with everything you've planned for them. And with you personally."

There's the snag, thought Claudia. I'd have to be responsible directly to this perfectionist; there's no way I could satisfy him, and he would take pleasure in finding fault with my methods and humiliating me. And suppose the German ladies were difficult—if they're very rich, they probably are. I'm not really as

patient as he thinks I am. Then something else occurred to her.

"What would you be doing with these ladies if I
hadn't walked into your office this evening?" she asked.

Huntley Fox smiled a wan smile. "A good question.
I had already decided to try and keep the husbands
and wives together as much as possible and send them
on the regular tours, with the men acting as inter-
preters. If none of the men wanted to go, I would have
had to send Anton along—but I want to avoid that. He
could be very unsatisfactory in many ways with a
group of rich German ladies who are genuinely interested in Balinese culture. The husbands would mostly
be bored, I suspect, and their report on Bali Breezes
not very good. By employing you as I've outlined, we
will, I hope, send them home with a far better impression. In addition to your room and board and the
drivers to take you around, starting tomorrow, this is
the salary I'll pay you for the week."

He scribbled a figure on a piece of paper and pushed
it across the desk to her. Claudia could hardly believe
her eyes when she saw it. It was an executive salary
such as she had never dreamed of.

"This amount?" she said. "For one week's work? I
can't turn *that* down."

"Good. But it'll be a hard week. By the way, I'll
want you to dine in the private dining room with me
and the whole German party each of the four evenings
they'll be here. And to come with us to the nightclub
on the top floor or to the native dance or whatever
they want to do afterward. You will be acting almost in
the capacity of . . . of hostess for me. I won't want
you to let me down."

"I'll do my best," said Claudia, her mind still bog-
gling at what she would be paid. "Shall I report to
you tomorrow?"

"Yes. At nine o'clock in the morning. I'll have a car and driver ready for you. You should already have a plan mapped out for the day. And equip yourself with a suitable wardrobe for when the guests arrive."

"I'll do that," she replied vaguely. She got up from her chair and started toward the door. "Thank you very much, Mr. Fox."

"By the way," he called after her, "two more things. First, if you prove satisfactory, I might continue the arrangement on a more permanent basis. Second, as you're to be my official hostess so to speak, we should appear to be on more . . . more . . . er, to know each other better than we actually do. It will make the evenings more comfortable for the guests. So you should call me by my first name, which is Huntley, and I will call you by yours. Gretchen, isn't it?"

An inexplicable blush crept up her neck onto her cheeks as she said, "No, it's Claudia. You . . . you can call me Claudia."

He smiled warmly for the first time since she had met him. It made him seem young, almost boyish, with his unruly lock drifting across his forehead. He stood up, ungainly in his great height, and looked for a moment like a shy college kid on a first date. If this is the real him, she thought, my lucky stars were working for me today when they brought me here. It might even be exciting to work for him, to be close to him for a few days.

"Good night . . . Huntley," she said, smiling back.

"Good night, Claudia. I'll phone down to the reception desk now, and tell them to send you back to Kuta in a taxi. Don't wait around for Anton; he'll have given up on you long ago."

"All right," she said. "I'll see you tomorrow." She walked out of the office, and shut the heavy door behind her. Then she leaned back against it for a minute, resting her head, her eyes closed, trying to recapitulate everything that had happened since she had first walked into that office. Finally, shaking her head in disbelief, her long blond hair rippling on her shoulders, she walked slowly to the bank of elevators, and pressed the button to take her down to the lobby.

It was impossible to appreciate that she was now an employee of this vast enterprise, that all the amenities of a luxury hotel were hers to enjoy in her spare time, and that she had a whopping salary into the bargain. It was even harder to realize that she was already on first-name, friendly terms with the cold, hard man she had first seen that afternoon directing his splendorous empire.

In spite of Huntley's prediction Anton was waiting for her in the lobby. He hurried up as soon as she stepped off the elevator, his fresh, good-looking face clouded with anxiety.

"What did he want with you, Claudia? The snake—I do not trust him. He works always behind the back."

"I don't know why you'd say that," she replied calmly. "He was offering me a job, that's all. On his personal staff."

"On *his* staff? I wanted you to be on my staff. What sort of a job does he offer you?"

Claudia didn't want to use the word *hostess* to Anton—it sounded too intimate somehow—so she told him that it was just a temporary position as a tour conductor for some German women who were arriving in a few days. She made as light of it as she could, and didn't mention the salary.

Anton mumbled some words of disapproval and then added more brightly, "Perhaps it is okay. After the week is finish, we will try again for the dancing exercise class for you. By then he will know you can be successful with the guests."

Fortunately Claudia didn't have to explain that there was a possibility of the position on the manager's staff being continued and that the prospect of working for him now registered in her mind as an exciting challenge rather than as a distasteful chore, for one of the reception clerks came up and told her that the taxi ordered by the manager was waiting for her outside.

"He is sending you home in a taxi?" Anton sounded outraged. "But I wait here so long for you, to drive you home myself."

"Sorry, Anton," she said gaily. "But I mustn't disobey the boss's orders before I've even started work. I'm moving in tomorrow. I expect I'll see you around."

Leaving him gaping on the doorstep, she ran out to the taxi and hopped in. Before midnight she was back in her little room in the guesthouse, grateful that this was to be her last night on the lumpy mattress. Soon she was asleep, her program for the next day only half-formulated and many questions about the new turn of events in her life still unanswered.

Shortly before nine the next morning she was back at the hotel, carrying her suitcase. She had found a clean blouse and skirt and had ironed them soon after dawn; recalling Huntley's deprecating remark about her loose hairstyle, she had done it up in a tight bun. When she arrived at the manager's office, she hoped she looked suitably efficient and businesslike to satisfy him.

The outer office was buzzing with activity this morning. Huntley's private secretary, a neatly groomed middle-aged American lady, greeted her with a broad smile. "You must be Miss Bauer," she said. "I'm Eleanor Davis, and if there's anything I can do for you, you just let me know. I must say I think it's real swell, his taking you on to help with the German visitors; I know he's been worrying about that."

"Thank you, Eleanor. And please call me Claudia. I was meant to see him at nine o'clock. Can I go in?"

"I'm afraid he's in conference this morning. But he left me this book for you"—Eleanor handed over a well-thumbed volume called, *The History and Arts of Bali*—"and this list of things for you to check out."

Claudia took the sheet with a dozen items neatly typed on it. They included, "Complete familiarity with the National Museum and its most interesting artifacts," "Full knowledge of the processes and products of the Mutiara Batik Factory," and "Conversant understanding of Indonesian cooking, with emphasis on Balinese specialties—see hotel's executive chef." The other items were equally comprehensive.

"Wow!" said Claudia. "I hope he doesn't expect me to become an expert on all these things in three days."

Eleanor smiled. "He does demand a lot from his staff, you know. But don't worry, dear. Just do the best you can. I'm sure you can cope with it all right. And when you need the car to take you around, speak to reception; I've arranged it with them for you."

"That's fine," said Claudia, still reeling slightly from the enormity of the task Huntley had set her. "By the way, do you know which is to be my room? I'll drop off my suitcase there before I start work."

"Oh, yes," replied Eleanor a little uncomfortably. "There was a spot of trouble over that. It seems that the reservations manager didn't have anything to spare this week. So we've put you in with the principal dancer—her name's Negara. I'm sure you'll manage all right; it's a nice big room with two beds. Mr. Fox was sorry about it—quite annoyed really—but there was nothing else that could be arranged on the spur of the moment."

Claudia took her suitcase to the room that Eleanor had described as Negara's, but there was a sign that read "Do not disturb" hanging on the doorknob. So Negara sleeps in late, she thought. I'd better not start things off badly by waking her up. Accordingly she left her suitcase with the room boy for that corridor and asked him to put it inside when Negara had surfaced for the day. With a mischievous smile, the boy took it and promised to do as she had said. His smile seemed to suggest that Huntley Fox wasn't the only one who was put out by the fact of Negara's having to share her room with Claudia.

Following Huntley's instructions, Claudia decided to investigate the museum first. Her driver brought a small black car to the hotel entrance. Claudia hopped in beside him, Huntley's book on Bali clutched in her hand. As they bumped down the road to Denpasar, the capital of the island, she opened it for the first time. The flyleaf had "Huntley Fox" inscribed in a bold hand at the top. She handled it with great care when she realized that it came from his personal collection.

The book was dry and technical, but it had an index, and Claudia decided the most efficient way to use it would be to look up references to exhibits she saw in the museum. That way she would be able to answer the German ladies' questions about what was on show. At the museum, however, she found that many of the objects were labeled only in Indonesian. This defeated her plan, and with a sigh she came to the conclusion that she would have to wade through the book and memorize descriptions of the huge stone sculptures and implements that surrounded her, so as to be able to identify them to her charges. That was a task better reserved for an evening at the hotel.

A row of carvings—men with flat noses and enormous blank eyes—were labeled "The Seven Heavenly Seers" according to the book, and there was a miniature representation of the gruesome tooth-pulling ceremony in which the village headman extracted the six upper front teeth of all boys and girls at puberty. She shuddered at the thought and made a note to ask Huntley if the practice had been discontinued.

Huntley gave the impression of boundless knowledge and total control of everything in his ken. What a remarkable man he was! Claudia found it hard to understand how anyone could be so consistently serious, so utterly absorbed in his work day and night.

Leaving the museum for a return visit when she was better informed, she told the driver to take her to the Mutiara Batik Factory. When she announced herself, Mr. Mutiara took great pains to demonstrate to her each of the complicated steps that created beautiful multicolored lengths of fabric from simple white cotton cambric. She watched rows of girls squatting in front of a low table, applying beeswax with a tiny brush to the parts that would later become brown or green or gold. The patterns were incredibly intricate and the brainchild of each individual worker. Then she saw the dyeing process by which the unwaxed parts took on a blue tint; this was followed by waxing over the blue parts and also scraping the wax off the parts to become brown before dipping the material in brown dye. This process was repeated with the green and gold until finally all the wax was removed with boiling water and the material hung out to dry.

Claudia learned that a really complicated pattern incorporating six or seven hues could take a girl as long as a whole year to produce. She saw one softly delicate length, only one meter wide by three meters long, for sale for a thousand dollars. If it had been done on silk, an even slower and more skillful procedure, it would have cost twice that amount, said Mr. Mutiara reverently, adding that the process involved was a hundred times more complex than the making of regular tourist dresses.

"Surely there is a quicker way of producing these patterns?" she asked, and Mr. Mutiara reluctantly took her to a shed at the back of his factory where some men with rubber stamps were coloring white cotton with designs by repeatedly pressing the stamp, dipped in dye, in rows across the cloth. The process took a fraction of the time to complete, but even Claudia's inexperienced eye could see that the result was far less appealing. It held none of the mystic charm of the true, hand-waxed dipping method. The prints were too perfectly symmetrical, lacking the tiny flaws and discrepancies that could be found in the genuine article.

"We make these stamped-out pieces for the local market—for the peasants to wear when they work in the fields," explained Mr. Mutiara. "Only the real batik is sold to the tourists."

At any rate, only the real batik is sold at the Bali Breezes Hotel, thought Claudia; this must be the inferior type banned by Huntley Fox.

Thanking Mr. Mutiara for his trouble, Claudia climbed back into the car and asked the driver to wait a moment while she made notes in a notebook she had brought with her. Considering the amount of information she had to collect in three days, she couldn't possibly retain it all in her head, and notes were a necessity. But the driver was in a chatty mood and insisted on talking while she wrote. She was only half listening until he mentioned the name of his village, Bedulu. Then she pricked up her ears because Bedulu was the place where the best Balinese dancers were reputed to come from; she had visited it several times while she was staying in her guesthouse at Kuta —the *boomi* ride had used up a whole dollar of her money each time—and had met and much enjoyed an old man called Tabanan, who had once been the guiding light of the informal village dancing school. He had taken an interest in Claudia, and had helped her greatly with her studies.

"Do you know an old man called Tabanan?" she asked the driver.

His face broke into a broad grin. "Tabanan, he is my cousin. He very excited now—all Bedulu very excited."

"What's the cause of the excitement?" asked Claudia.

"A new young dancer has come to the village. She come with her family from a distant part in the north of Bali. Tabanan say she is the best girl dancer he see for many years."

"When did she arrive?" Claudia asked. "I never heard anything about her when I was there about a week ago. In fact, Tabanan seemed unhappy because there wasn't any new talent coming along. He said the young people were giving up the traditional dances."

"This new dancer—her name is Penebel, so Tabanan tell me—come a few days ago, and already she has made the young men interested again. The dancing school is busy every day, and my cousin very pleased. We go there now, miss? We go now to Bedulu to see Tabanan and his new dancer?"

Claudia found the driver's suggestion extremely tempting. Although she was delving into aspects of Balinese culture not required for Huntley Fox's crash course, dancing was still her first love, and she wanted to hear about this encouraging new development. Besides, she rationalized to herself, it would be something unique and special to introduce to the visiting Germans. To see a performance under the stars on the makeshift platform they used as a stage up there would be a change from the more professional setup of the dances put on at the Bali Breezes. Surely Huntley would approve of that. She told the driver to take her to Bedulu.

The narrow road to the village wound through dense forest. Waterfalls plunged over rocks at the hairpin bends; native women could be seen washing their clothes in the pools below. Ornamental brick temples, decorated with weird stone figures and roofed with curving tiles, occupied small spaces hacked out of the jungle, each the central building of a hamlet. Ahead, reaching up into the sky, were the mountains, dark green and mysterious. Each time Claudia had made this journey, she had marveled at the living beauty of the scenery; it had for centuries inspired the inhabitants of the island to develop their own variations on the Hindu religion, and produce their own imaginative styles of legend, architecture, and visual arts, as well as their proverbial dances.

The driver stopped the car in front of a palm-thatched building that Claudia knew well. It was the home of her friend Tabanan, only a few doors from the dance platform. The old man himself was dozing in the afternoon heat, slumped in a rickety chair, a homemade straw hat pulled over his eyes.

"Tabanan!" cried Claudia's driver. "Wake up! I have brought a young lady to see you. She wants to hear about Penebel."

Tabanan pushed back his hat and blinked into the sunlight. "Ah! Claudia! I was hoping you would return soon to Bedulu. So you have already heard about the treasure we have been sent? For too long bad fortune has fallen on us; even the Rangda,"—he pointed at the grotesque mask with lolling tongue and three feet of straw hair that hung at the entrance to his house— "even the Rangda has been unable to keep the evil spirits out."

"But now that you have a new dancer, things are looking up?" she asked.

"As they have not for many years. Come with me."

They walked together down the dusty path to where the stage had been set up in front of a crumbling, half-overgrown temple. To one side, two men were beating out a strange, sad melody on the loose brass plates of their xylophones. It twanged across the compound, compelling in its insistent rhythm, and half a dozen young men, bare from the waist up, were swaying their hips and arms in time with the music. But their eyes were glued to the source of their inspiration, a short, curvaceous girl with coal-black hair and dark brown skin, dressed simply in a long skirt and white T-shirt, who moved with a fluid grace as though her body were made of rubber.

Penebel executed her dance with a faultless precision that Claudia had never before witnessed. She flicked through the scissors movement of her fingers so fast that they became a blur. Toward the end she splayed and crossed her feet in a difficult step that took her sideways across the stage; with other dancers it usually turned into a series of awkward hops; Penebel made it into a glide. Her performance was stunning, even in simple clothes. In costume it would have been breathtaking.

When the music died down, Penebel stood quietly, as if slowly coming out of a trance. Then she smiled at Tabanan, and ran down to meet him and be introduced to Claudia. "I think I was better today," she said modestly.

Tabanan laid a wrinkled hand kindly on her shoulder. "You were very good today," he said. "Don't you think so, Claudia?"

"I thought you were marvelous," replied Claudia sincerely. "How old are you, Penebel?"

"Seventeen," said the girl. "By the time I am twenty, I hope to be the best in Bali."

"Are you going to put on a proper show next week?" Claudia asked Tabanan. "If so, I would like to bring some friends to watch. They would pay money to help with your costumes."

"What friends are these?" asked Tabanan suspiciously.

"They are visitors—from the Bali Breezes Hotel."

Tabanan grinned at Penebel. "Then they do have plenty of money, and it is true that we need some new costumes. As you know, usually we dance only for the village, and for our friends such as Claudia here—not for payment. But what do you say, my child, shall we put on the *ramayana* ballet for these rich people who Claudia will bring?"

"Oh, let's!" said Penebel with glee. "I love the *ramayana*. And I would like them to see that I can dance as well as that light-skinned girl who dances at the hotel."

"I would like them to see that too," smiled Claudia. "And I would particularly like the hotel manager to see it. It might lift the scales from his eyes."

"What is that you say?" asked Tabanan sharply. "I have not heard about the light-skinned girl. Is she more good than Penebel?"

"No," said Claudia. "Frankly she's not. But she is tall and very beautiful, and the hotel manager worships the ground she walks on. That doesn't matter to me, but I think he should be disillusioned about her dancing ability. It gives her an unfair advantage."

"Advantage over what? Over you perhaps?" The old man peered at Claudia mischievously.

Claudia tossed her head back abruptly. "No, of course not. I meant . . . I meant over the other dancers in the team. I work for him now . . . but that's all.

54

I just want some hotel guests to see the genuine Balinese style performed by real Balinese dancers. I'll try and arrange to bring them all up here next week to see your pupils do the *ramayana* ballet. And the manager too, if I can persuade him."

On the way back to the hotel Claudia wondered how she was going to get Huntley to allow her to include a trip to Bedulu in her program for the German ladies; he would be possessive about Negara and the hotel's own dance group. And how was she going to see that he came too to watch Penebel? She wondered, also, what he would think when he saw Penebel dance. Would his avowed appreciation of quality overcome his personal bias toward Negara? It would be interesting to see. . . .

Late in the afternoon her driver dropped her off at the hotel. She was hot and dusty from all her traveling, and the large open-air swimming pool beckoned.

Claudia remembered that her swimsuit was still in her suitcase up in Negara's room, but it was too faded and out of style for the elegant crowd around the pool. With her new salary assured she could afford something more appropriate, so she went straight to one of the boutiques in the lobby and bought herself a cute batik bikini that fit perfectly. Wearing it, she walked confidently out to the pool, carrying her clothes, notebook, and Huntley's volume in one of the boutique's plastic bags.

This is the life, she thought, stretching out in the sun on a beach chair, idly watching the bronzed young men and women who splashed and laughed, or lazed around the edge, soaking up the rays and sipping cold drinks. Beyond the pool's grass verge, a beach of coarse sand sloped down to the breakers. She felt relaxed and content.

Claudia was contemplating a plunge into the clear

blue swimming pool when Anton came up to her. In his T-shirt last night he had looked muscular; now, in a pair of brief trunks, he looked like Mr. Universe. The cultivation of that physique must take him hours each day, she thought.

"Claudia!" he exclaimed, dropping onto his haunches beside her chair. "All the day I search for you. But you are nowhere to see. So in my office this afternoon I think you must be behind the door in Huntley's office. What is it that you do in there?"

"Anton, you're imagining things," she said. "As a matter of fact, I haven't even seen him all day. He just left me written instructions. I've been chasing round the countryside since nine o'clock, trying to become an expert on Bali in three days. I've only just quit."

Anton shook his head in disgust. "It will be better when this week is over and you come to work for me. Then you will take your class each morning, and for the rest of the day you can have the leisure. And I will have some leisure with you."

"We'll see," said Claudia noncommittally.

"This evening we will dine together," announced Anton. "And after, we will find some amusement, yes?"

"I'll be glad to have dinner at your table," said Claudia, for she was not looking forward to eating alone, "but afterward I'm afraid I have a lot of homework to do. I have an exam to pass, you know."

At that moment they both became aware of a whirring noise in the space above them. It grew quickly louder, a thunderous roar descending from the sky. Then her eye caught a helicopter skimming over the roof of the hotel. Its huge blades chopping through the air, it poised motionless for a second over a circular concrete platform that jutted out between the beachside palms into the sea. Then the ungainly machine dropped down, hesitating momentarily over the platform before settling gently in its exact center.

The motor was turned off and the door opened. Out came the youngest of the three Arabs Claudia had seen yesterday; he turned to assist the other two down the steps onto the concrete. Clutching their headdresses and long robes, they stood unsteadily on the ground. Whatever experience they had had in the helicopter obviously had unnerved them somewhat; in fact, they looked thoroughly distressed.

Then the pilot climbed out and started herding his passengers down the jetty toward where Claudia sat. She couldn't help marveling at the skill and daring with which he had handled the machine, bringing it so close over the hotel to a pinpoint landing. The noise of its motor was still ringing in her ears when she saw that the pilot, wearing a spotless white jumpsuit, bore the unmistakable tall figure of Huntley Fox himself. His lock of dark hair dangled, as usual, over his forehead, but he wasn't wearing his glasses, and his eyes were dancing with pleasure as he cracked a joke with the youngest Arab. It was hard to believe that this was the same dour-faced hotel manager she had met last night.

The revelation that this hero of the skies was the man for whom she was to work for the next seven days had a curiously unsettling effect on Claudia. Her pulse began to quicken as the foursome came down the jetty; they would have to pass within a few feet of where she sat with Anton still crouching on the ground beside her. If he spoke to her as he passed, she felt that she would jump and probably giggle nervously, like a schoolgirl presented to a pop idol.

But Huntley didn't speak to her as he led the Arabs

past her chair. He looked, his smile wiped out for a moment by a glance that encompassed both her and Anton, and then passed on.

"Too much awful noise, that machine it makes," said Anton.

Claudia had been about to reply when she realized that Huntley Fox had stopped in his tracks and turned around. He was waving the Arabs on into the hotel and was calling her to come to him. She got up from her chair and went toward him, her heart thudding, shamefully aware of the minimal coverage afforded by her bikini.

CHAPTER FOUR

Huntley Fox made no move to meet her, but stood waiting for her to come up to him. Her dance training helped her to walk naturally, neither too fast nor too slow; she hoped it hid the uneasiness she felt. She sensed that all eyes from around the pool were focused on her.

At last she stood before Huntley, sweeping her wind-blown hair back from her face. The jocular expression he had worn when he first climbed out of the aircraft had vanished; his dark, inscrutable eyes swept over her body for a moment before he spoke.

"Good afternoon, Claudia," he said.

"Good afternoon, Mr. Fox," she answered brightly. "I mean good afternoon, Huntley."

A tiny smile flickered on his lips. "You look more like a guest at the hotel than an employee."

The smile had given her courage. "And you look more like a helicopter pilot than a hotel manager."

"I don't deny that it's a role I prefer. But even when flying the chopper, I'm doing my job. I took the Arabs up to see the crater of the volcano. But they seemed more concerned with their own safety than with the beauty of the boiling lava."

"The older ones did look rather scared when they came down," she said. "I can't think why they would be; I'm sure you're a very careful pilot."

"I like to think so, but the first party I took up there was also a bit frightened. I'm trying to make up my mind whether to offer it as a regular attraction to the guests."

"I think it would be marvelous—a real thrill for them."

"In that case, I'll take you on an experimental trip to the crater one day soon. Then, if you don't lose your cool, I'll try it on some more groups of guests, ladies too."

"I'd love that," she said, her hazel eyes glinting at the thought of soaring into the sky with him. "When can we go?"

"Some day when I have time. My schedule is tighter than yours, it seems. I see you were enjoying the sun with Anton Reinholtz. Surely you haven't completed that list of assignments I left for you this morning?"

His biting tone unnerved her, but she managed an easy laugh. "Not in one day, no. But I made a good start on it. It'll be more than enough to keep me busy tomorrow and the next day."

"I intended it to be. That's why I'm surprised to see you lounging around the pool with Anton."

"I'd only just come back from the drive up to

Bedulu," she protested, stung by his sarcasm. "I was taking a few minutes off before going upstairs to read your book."

"Bedulu?" he repeated, staring malevolently at her. "I wasn't aware that Bedulu was on the list of places I told you to visit."

Claudia bit her lip. Why did she have to go and let that cat out of the bag? "I . . . I went up to the dancing school there. It's run by a friend of mine, and I wanted to see their fabulous new girl dancer. I . . . I thought perhaps the German guests . . ."

"We have our own fabulous girl dancer at this hotel," he cut in, glaring down at her. "I thought you saw her last night at the *kecak* dance. Or maybe you only had eyes for your escort."

Claudia forced herself to ignore this last snide remark. "Negara? Oh, yes, she's very good, but . . ."

"But nothing. In future you will stick to your assignments, do you understand?"

She cast her eyes to the ground penitently, and rubbed her toe on the grass. "Yes, Mr. Fox."

"My name is Huntley," he said more softly. "And talking of Negara, it's a pity we've had to put you in to share her room; I'm afraid she'll be unhappy about that. But you'll find her a very pleasant person to be with."

"As does your Uncle Wilbur, I hear." Claudia immediately regretted her remark, for the manager looked at her more stonily than ever.

"So you have heard about that already. I might have known."

"It was just gossip . . ."

"Unfortunately it's a lot more important than that," said Huntley. "I'd prefer that you keep it to yourself. If you're sharing a room with Negara, she might let something slip . . ."

"Oh, I'll be the soul of discretion, don't worry."

"Good, I'll appreciate that. Now I must go and change; I have work to do. And so do you." He glanced at the gold, multipurpose watch on his long, lean wrist. "You haven't yet told me what you did do today that was in accordance with my instructions, but there isn't time now. Why don't you come to my office at eight this evening, and I'll make sure you're on the right track. I'll be having some dinner sent up at that time— I'll order some for you too, and we can talk while we eat. That way I won't be wasting any time."

"Thank you very much," she said. "I'll look forward to it."

"It will be a business discussion," he reminded her harshly. "Not the kind of dinner for two such as you are probably used to having with your male companions."

Claudia felt herself blushing, "No . . . no, I understand that." She wanted to get away from him now before he spotted her confusion. "I'll see you at eight, then—in your office. I—I'll bring my notebook."

She turned and ran across the grass to Anton, without even looking back to see whether Huntley had watched her lissome figure bound away from him. For some strange reason, she hoped he had . . .

As she had expected, Anton was annoyed by the manager's interruption of their chat. "Why he not leave you alone?" Anton complained. "It was not important, what he say to you, I am sure."

"He just wanted to know how I'd got on today. It's understandable that he would. After all, it is my first day on the job."

Anton jumped from his sitting position on the ground onto the balls of his feet as if doing a gymnastic exercise. Not content with that exhibition of athletic prowess, he bounced on his toes a few times as if skipping, before coming to rest beside where she stood. His intention to impress her was evident, but Claudia found herself singularly unmoved.

"I think he want to inspect your body, no more," said Anton. "For that I have no blame for him. Your body very nice. You like my body too?" He flexed his biceps for her, and the pectorals on his chest stood out like iron as well.

"Er, yes . . . yes, it's very powerful," said Claudia. "But now I'm afraid you'll have to find some other girl to show it off to, as I must go up to my room to do some work." She started to move toward the hotel.

"Okay, so you want to be the slave—so be the slave! But I warn you, my Claudia, the more for him you do, the more he want you to do. At first with me he was like that, but not anymore. Now Anton please himself, and Huntley Fox not bother him."

"How do you get away with it, Anton?" she asked.

"Aha!" he replied with a smirk. "Anton not be fired by Huntley, not ever fired. Uncle Wilbur see to that. Uncle Wilbur Anton's friend."

"So that's your secret," laughed Claudia. "Well, I must go."

"I will see you in the bar for a drink before our dinner?"

"Oh, I'm sorry, Anton," she said. "I forgot to tell you. The manager has invited me to eat in his office with him. To talk business."

"Since when he invite you?" Anton's eyebrows shot up angrily.

"Since just now. And I simply couldn't refuse. You must see that it's part of my job. We'll meet for dinner another night."

Anton shrugged his massive shoulders. "It is as you wish." He strolled away toward the pool, his pride plainly damaged. He'll get over it, she thought.

She collected a key for Negara's room from the desk, and went up the elevator, still in her bikini. It felt odd, but marvelously decadent, to be wandering around this luxurious building in a swimsuit, but she had seen the guests do it, so assumed it was acceptable.

She unlocked the door of Negara's room and went in. It was a beautiful big room; glass doors opened onto a private balcony that overlooked the pool and the row of palm trees partitioning it from the sea. There were two beds, each fitted with a heavy bedspread, a built-in dresser and wardrobe, and two comfortable chairs beside a low coffee table. It was the most sumptuous hotel bedroom Claudia had ever seen.

When Claudia entered, Negara was sitting at the dressing table, arranging her long, dark tresses into a ponytail. She turned around and smiled, and in that instant Claudia began to understand the compelling attraction she had for both Wilbur Fox and his nephew. Offstage she was more beautiful than on it; Western clothes suited her far better than Balinese costume. Her large green eyes, heavy with mascara, shone like a Siamese cat's, and the sensuous curve of her oriental lips was enough to make any man catch his breath.

Negara looked Claudia over with interest but no apparent hostility. "So you're Anton's new girl friend? His taste is improving. I'm glad to meet you, Claudia."

"I'm glad to meet you too, Negara." Claudia smiled back at the dusky goddess at the dressing table. "But I'm not Anton's girl friend. Is that what he's been saying?"

"He hinted at it this morning. But Anton tends to get carried away. When he first brought me here from Jakarta, he told all and sundry that I was the girl he had always been waiting for."

"How did you put him straight? I might need to use the same tactics if he doesn't let up on me soon."

"I let it be clearly seen that I preferred someone else, the great Wilbur Fox, to be precise. Now Anton and I are just good friends. He did me a good turn by bringing me here to meet Wilbur, and I did him one by coming. Wilbur is grateful to him for that, you see."

Claudia thought this over for a minute. "So it's the uncle you're fond of, Negara? Somehow I thought it was his nephew, Huntley . . ."

Negara laughed, a rippling laugh that was accompanied by a toss of her ponytail. "Poor Huntley," she said. "Yes, I'm afraid he would like it to be that way, although the dear, gangly man is too shy ever to have made a pass at me. I prefer older men."

"But Huntley must be thirty-two at least . . ."

"I mean much older men—men with real substance, like Wilbur. Huntley will go on being no more than a hotel manager for some years yet, moving from one part of the world to another on two-year stints, while Wilbur already owns the whole chain. He can live in California and travel as much as he likes. That's the life for me. By the way, I hope you have your own room by the time he arrives. It might be awkward . . ."

"It's very unlikely I'll still be here by then," said Claudia. "Huntley's only taken me on for a week to entertain some special guests."

"You believe that story?" Negara laughed again, and rose like the image of Venus from her chair to smooth the jacket of her suit in front of the mirror. In her high heels, she was several inches taller than Claudia, as slender and statuesque as a fashion model. With that figure she could be a showgirl in an American nightclub, thought Claudia, but never a Balinese dancer.

But what had she said about Claudia's job not being what she thought it was?

"What do you mean, Negara? I know my job as tour conductor wasn't Anton's original idea, but that's what Huntley's given me."

"Don't you see that it's only a cover-up?" asked Negara, her green eyes twinkling with sophisticated amusement. "A nice cover-up for Huntley himself. He's finally got wind of the gossip about his infatuation for me, and so he intends to use you as a diversion. He wants everyone to think he's interested in you; he's going to arrange to be seen about in public with you, being very attentive I've no doubt. But it's simply to put people off the scent about his feelings for me. So don't be taken in by it, Claudia; he's a clever manipulator, our Huntley Fox."

"I don't believe you," said Claudia, watching Negara continue to admire herself in the mirror from every angle. "He . . . he's not that kind of person. All he thinks about is his business. He wouldn't use one of his employees to do what you said."

"You're too naive, Claudia," replied Negara. "You're not a regular employee, as you yourself told me. You were taken on staff especially for the purpose I mentioned. And as soon as his problem with me is resolved one way or the other—of course he hopes that I'll agree to marry him—you'll be fired. But actually it'll be the other way—as soon as Wilbur carries me off to the States. Huntley will be brokenhearted of course, but I can't help that. Anyway you'll no longer be needed, so your job will come abruptly to an end. I'm only telling you this for your own good. I wouldn't want you to be hurt."

"You've no proof . . ." Claudia began, in spite of an uneasy feeling in the pit of her stomach. Almost anything might be true of such a strange man.

"Haven't I? I was watching you by the pool. Didn't he call you over for a cozy chitchat just when everyone was watching him after landing that infernal machine of his? And Eleanor, his secretary, has let it out that you're to be his chummy hostess at private dinner parties. I'll bet he's even asked you to have dinner with him tonight—alone!"

Claudia's scalp prickled under the strain of listening to Negara's theory—and, worse, her evidence. But Huntley's invitation to eat with him in his office this evening was purely between him and her, not a public exhibition. "You're right," she said. "He did ask me to his office for some supper, but nobody knows about that; it's entirely a private affair. So you see . . ."

"You haven't told anybody about it? Not even Anton?"

"Well, I did tell Anton, yes. I had to put off a date with him. He didn't take it too well, as a matter of fact."

"Exactly," shrugged Negara. "And Anton will tell everyone else. The whole hotel will know. It won't be as private as you think."

"I still can't believe it. Not a man like Huntley Fox . . ."

"After you've had your little snack in his office, he'll probably parade you through the hotel, holding your hand or some such tender gesture. Well, I must go; I'm meeting a charming Japanese gentleman this evening—I have to fill in my time somehow until Wilbur gets here. Don't wait up for me. And have a good time this evening. Remember not to be fooled by Huntley's attentions. Just enjoy them."

Negara picked up a delicate evening bag and headed for the door, leaving Claudia standing in the middle of the room.

Claudia stared at her unpacked suitcase, and at the disarray of discarded clothes and personal belongings that her roommate had left strewn across the room. Was there any truth in what Negara had said? Was she being used as a decoy for the manager's true feelings? If so, the best thing for her to do would be to take her suitcase and flee from the hotel right now. She wasn't the sort of girl to play along lightly, as Negara seemed to expect her to do. Her indefinable attraction toward Huntley made that impossible, quite apart from the matter of her pride.

She sat down on the bed to think. A shiver ran through her body, but whether it was because she was too scantily dressed for the air conditioning or for another reason, she couldn't tell. At last she stood up and started unpacking. She had come to a decision. If, after dinner, Huntley did "parade her through the hotel" as Negara had predicted he would, she would pack up and leave tomorrow. If, on the other hand, he simply sent her back to her room to study his book, as she expected him to do, she would stay on and see what happened. How she longed to prove to Negara that she was totally wrong! She wanted so much to believe that Huntley was the upright, straightforward man that she believed him to be, not the clever manipulator that both Anton and Negara accused him of being.

Precisely at eight she went to the manager's office. She was wearing the same batik sundress that she had worn the night before, simply because it was the only pretty dress she had. She had debated with herself what to do with her hair and had decided on a compromise between the severe and the loose styles; she had it rolled up in a neat pageboy at the nape of her neck. Her makeup, however, was a little heavier than usual;

if he liked the elaborate accentuation that Negara applied to her naturally alluring eyes, he wouldn't object to her less dramatic artifice.

She was surprised to find Huntley's office door open. Was someone else already there? Someone to witness her arrival and report it around the hotel? She knocked on the door and peeked around it at the same time. Apart from Huntley himself, the room was empty. She felt ashamed of herself for being so suspicious, but the seeds of doubt had been firmly planted by Negara; Claudia was pleased to find that Huntley passed the first test at least.

He was seated in one of the soft chairs by the coffee table, wearing a crisp, open-necked shirt and white cord pants. His feet were slipped comfortably into sandals. His glasses were on the table beside him, although he was reading some typewritten sheets. That's funny, she thought. He doesn't need them for flying, nor for reading. What does he use them for?

"Come in, Claudia," he said, motioning to a chair beside him. "Excuse my clothes, but I'm not expecting any official business tonight, and it's good to get out of uniform once in a while."

"I'm glad you can," she said. "I see you're not wearing your glasses. Don't you need them for reading?" She slipped easily into the chair he indicated; the informality of his appearance and of his greeting made her feel more comfortable.

He smiled, that warm disarming smile that set her pulse quickening as it had before. "You're very observant. It just shows how relaxed I feel; I forgot to put them on when you came in. I usually don't let anyone see me without them when I'm working; I think they improve my image."

"You don't really need them at all, then?"

"No, they're plain glass. See for yourself if you don't

believe me." He handed the heavy-rimmed spectacles to her to examine. "But promise not to tell anybody. It's my only guilty secret."

Is it really his only one? she wondered. Negara's accusations were terrible, amounting to a particularly wanton form of deception. Suppose she fell for him—it might not be hard to do—then he would have toyed with her affections in the worst way, purely for his own business reasons. Although somewhat reassured by his comfortable presence this evening, she determined to keep her guard up.

"Yes, it's foolish of me, I suppose," he went on. "But I don't really have the temperament to be a hotel manager, so I have to use little tricks—like the glasses. Well, that's more than enough about me; tell me how you got on today—before you started branching out on your own and taking off for Bedulu." Although the reference grated on her, Claudia sensed that his annoyance had evaporated.

As she described her experience in the museum and at the batik factory, he got up silently and ambled across the room to a built-in closet containing a food warmer. Presently he returned with a tray of steak and vegetables, which he set before them on the low table. There was a bottle of red wine to go with the meal.

Claudia paused in her account to say, "That looks delicious, Huntley. I haven't had steak since I left home."

"Yes, I hanker for a bit of good American food sometimes, even though I enjoy Indonesian cooking. By the way, I had this sent up ahead of time, rather than have a waiter bring it up while you were here. I, er, didn't want anybody disturbing us this evening. They might get the wrong idea, if you know what I mean. Gossip can be very destructive in a closed institution like this one."

"I suppose it can," she said, trying to appear as though the possibility had never occurred to her.

"Yes, I wouldn't want you to be put to any embarrassment." He poured out a glass of wine for each of them, and chewed thoughtfully on his steak. "There may be some talk as it is, since we'll be thrown together a certain amount as part of your job, but don't take any notice of it. If any such nonsense comes to my ears, I assure you I'll squash it immediately. I'll expect you to do the same."

"Of course," she said, her mind racing to piece together the meaning of his words. Negara had said he was deliberately trying to encourage gossip about himself and Claudia; yet here he was, apparently doing everything he could to prevent it. Was this just another of his wily tricks, she wondered, aimed at getting her to drop her guard until he chose some fateful moment to fan the flames of the gossip he said he wished to avoid? How devious was this man? Or wasn't he devious at all? More than anything in the world, as they sat there quietly eating their dinner, she wished that she could trust him completely.

Huntley expressed satisfaction at Claudia's knowledge of the batik industry, but was not so pleased at the progress she had made at the museum. "You'll have to read that book I lent you until you can identify each object and describe it intelligently," he said. "There's a glossary of Indonesian names at the back. You'll have to work out the German equivalents."

"Yes," she said humbly. "I'd better go and start on that now. Thank you very much for the steak. I really enjoyed it."

"Before you go, Claudia," he said, "there's something I'd like to show you downstairs. From it you can learn a little about contemporary Bali and our problems here; it will help you understand the history better. Come on, I'll take you down through the hotel."

Claudia's heart sank. So he *is* going to take me through the lobby and everywhere after all, she thought. He *does* want us to be seen together; Negara was right. I'll have to leave tomorrow as I'd promised myself. I refuse to allow myself to be made an utter fool of by this selfish, scheming man. I won't!

She looked at him, holding the door for her, his stray lock of hair drifting over one eye, his glasses forgotten on the table, casual in his sandals and slacks. As he smiled at her beckoningly, it was so hard to believe that he was anything but a lovable personality that her resolve almost melted. But she held fast to it, and passed through the door ahead of him, her chin held high and her eyes blazing with indignation.

"We'll go down the back stairs so as to avoid being seen," he said when they reached the corridor, and led the way down the deserted fire exit. A door at the bottom brought them into a darkened garden at the back of the hotel. "This way—follow me," he said quietly, taking a sandy path through the undergrowth. Uncomprehending, she followed his long, catlike strides until they skirted the fence that marked the edge of the hotel property and came out onto the moonlit beach. Not a soul had seen them for the whole distance.

The well-raked sand of the hotel beach stretched away to their right, with the ten stories of lighted windows rising behind it. To their left was more beach, still in its natural state; coconut fronds lying where they had fallen from the tall palms above—coconuts too, half buried in their green husks; and hardy, arid weeds struggling for existence in the sandy soil. Night birds called and mysterious rustlings could be heard from the thick jungle behind. The course of nature here had been undisturbed since the beginning of time. Claudia thought it was much more beautiful than the manicured hotel grounds. She stood for a moment in the stillness, listening to the sparkling waves plop gently onto the golden sand, watching the glade of moonlight ripple far out into the ocean, drinking in the charm of the whole primeval scene. In the ever-lasting serenity of this place, all ugly thoughts vanished from her mind.

"I see you like it here," Huntley's soft voice came from beside her. "So do I. I come here often when I want to escape from the commercial world of the hotel."

"It's lovely . . ." she breathed.

"Yes. It would be a shame to spoil it, wouldn't it? And yet that's just what my Uncle Wilbur wants to do. He wants to buy this piece of land and expand the hotel."

"And you don't want him to, is that it?"

"No, I don't. It's not that I don't want him to add more rooms—that would provide more jobs for the local people and contribute to the general prosperity of the island. It's because I don't want this particular piece of property to be disturbed."

"I can see why." She smiled up at his worried features. "It would destroy your personal haven of retreat."

"It's not even that. There are dozens of miles of natural beach like this all along the coast. It's because of what there is a few hundred yards further on. Come on, I'll show you."

He led the way along the fringe of the jungle, stepping easily over fallen logs and tiny rivulets. Claudia followed, trying to place her footsteps where his had been so as to avoid tripping over obstacles, until some dim lights began to show through the trees. A number of thatched houses, built up on stilts by the seashore, appeared out of the shadows. Several outrigger canoes were drawn up on the beach, their red-and-yellow striped sails flapping idly in the cool evening breeze. This was a small fishing village, as far removed in life-style from the hotel as if it had been a thousand miles away.

"If the hotel expands," Huntley explained as they came to a stop at the edge of the village, "it will come right up to where we are standing now. Think what that would do to the people who live here. It would destroy their peaceful way of life entirely."

"But, as you said, it would help their prosperity."

"These people don't need help; they are self-sufficient and happy doing their fishing and buying everything they need from the proceeds. They just want to be left alone. I know, because some of them have become friends of mine, and I've asked them."

"Friends of yours?" Claudia echoed in amazement. It was hard to imagine the powerful hotel manager hobnobbing with humble fisherfolk.

"You're surprised?" he smiled. "I suppose it is surprising that they would accept me as they have. But they're warm hearted people and they don't hold it against me that I work for the hotel."

"They know who you are, then?"

"Yes. I tried not to tell them, but some of their daughters work at Bali Breezes, and they found out anyway. I find their simple honesty and acceptance of what we would call poverty most refreshing after dealing all day with spoiled, demanding customers."

"It must be maddening for you. Why do you do it, Huntley?" she asked.

"That's another story," he replied enigmatically. "Let's have a cup of coffee at their little restaurant.

It's not very grand, but it serves the village as a meeting place."

They picked their way along the shoreline past the boats. "Sometimes," he said wistfully, "they take me out fishing with them early in the morning in their *jukungs*—that's their name for their sailing canoes— but I've been too tired to get up at dawn lately."

Huntley took a rough track up from the beach into the cluster of houses. One of them had a wooden platform built onto the front of it; two kerosene lamps swung from convenient branches above, and there were three tables and a dozen chairs. They made their way up some rickety steps and sat down.

"The lady who runs this place makes the most delicious *soto* in Bali. That's fish and chicken soup with dumplings in it, if you haven't tried it. She charges five cents a bowl, and I swear it's better than the kind my hotel chef makes and sells for a dollar. I told him that once. He was furious." Huntley smiled at the recollection, and Claudia found herself laughing with him. The hidden qualities of the manager were astounding her more every minute.

A wiry man, his chin grizzled with several days' growth of beard, came and sat down with them. He was dressed in a loincloth hitched up between his legs and no other clothes. His broad, dark-skinned feet were bare, and he placed each foot solidly on the floor as if used to keeping his balance on a rocking boat. He greeted Huntley with a friendly tap and a few unintelligible words, staring openly at Claudia as he said them.

Huntley answered him briefly in the same tongue, and then turned to Claudia. "He says you are a *bulan purnama*—that means a beautiful lady. He wants to know if you are my *ratu*—or queen."

The proprietor of the restaurant, who was now

74

hovering over them, apparently scolded the man for his impertinence, and some banter ensued. Huntley spoke slowly and deliberately in Indonesian, his slow Boston accent quite different from the natives' slurred chatter, but he made himself understood. Claudia wondered when he had found the time to learn this unusual language. Did the man ever sleep?

"*Tuan hamba yang cantik itu*," Huntley's friend pronounced with finality.

"What does that mean?" asked Claudia.

"He says in that case it is my daughter who is beautiful," replied Huntley.

"Did you say I was your daughter?" asked Claudia with horror.

"Well, I had to say something . . . he wouldn't accept that you were a *kawan*—a friend," Huntley said, rather sheepishly.

"Why didn't you say I was one of your employees? That's what I am, aren't I?"

"I don't know. I guess I wasn't thinking of you in that way."

"I'm glad to hear it," muttered Claudia under her breath; it was the best news she had heard all evening. Yet the suspicion suddenly leaped up and nagged her that he might have brought her here with the express intention of the story of their romantic walk leading back to the hotel. Some of the village girls worked there, didn't they? She did her best to shove the awful doubt to the back of her mind, but it persisted throughout the cup of coffee that she sipped in silence while the two men talked in words she couldn't understand.

"*Selamat dirgahayau*," said Huntley to the man when their conversation was over. "I was wishing him a happy, long life," he told Claudia. "It's time we were going back."

75

"Tell me something," said Claudia as they made their way back down to the beach. "Have you ever brought anyone else from the hotel out here?" She paused and then added, "Negara for instance?"

"Negara?" he said, stopping still in his tracks. "Why did you bring her name up?" He spoke her name reverently, as if it were sacred.

"Oh," she replied, trying to sound casual, "just because she's a pretty girl and works in the hotel. I merely wondered if you made a habit of bringing people out for a stroll like this in the evening."

"I see," he said, sounding relieved, and continuing their walk. "No, I've never brought anyone here before, if you want to know—especially not Negara. She prefers the bright lights. She wouldn't be able to see the difference between this and the Jakarta slum where she was brought up. This would certainly be no place to bring a gorgeous, sophisticated woman like Negara. But I didn't think you'd mind—you're not the same type at all."

"What type do you think I am, then?"

"I don't know," he replied evasively. "I haven't given it much thought. But you're certainly not in the same class as Negara."

They walked on in silence after that, plodding through the soft sand. Claudia was working through several different interpretations of his last remark.

Suddenly a black shadow, a foot across, popped out of a hole in front of her and scurried down into the foam with a curious hissing noise. Claudia screamed and clutched Huntley's arm.

"What was that?" she cried. "I nearly stepped on it."

"Only a crab," he said, laughing. "The beach is full of them at this time of night. They're more scared of you than you should be of them. Here, we'll walk in the water. You won't notice them there." He slipped an arm around her waist and guided her down to where the lapping waves were ankle-deep.

They splashed slowly along toward the hotel, his arm still holding her firmly. Unconsciously her own arm reached up and gripped the back of his belt; the closeness of their bodies started a fearful tumult inside her chest, and the swing of his thighs against her side gave her a sense not only of security but of overwhelming personal protection as well. It filled her with a sensation of illicit pleasure, and she knew she wanted more of it.

The end of the beach came all too quickly. They moved up out of the water onto the wet sand and passed into the hotel precincts. Huntley stopped, his arm still around her waist. She looked up at him expectantly.

"I think this is where we should say good night," he whispered. "We wouldn't want anyone to see us like this, would we?"

"No," she said in a very small voice.

"Well, good night, then, Claudia," he spoke in a firm tone now. "You can find your way back to your room, I'm sure. Report to me after you've seen the chef and done the other things I told you. Another instruction: Pick up your salary check from my secretary tomorrow and buy yourself some new clothes. I want you to look smart for our German guests when they arrive."

Then he was gone into the shadows, loping around the back of the hotel like a great jungle cat returning satisfied to its lair. Or was he more like the wily hunter going home after setting some deadly trap? She wished she knew. She would have to wait and see whether the story of their excursion together worked its way round through the various levels of the hotel staff until it came to Negara's ears. Then, if it had been a trap, Claudia would hear about it from her roommate soon enough.

As Claudia had expected, Negara was still out when Claudia let herself into their room. She took off the dress that Huntley had complimented her on last night but had not appreciated tonight. Did he tire easily of things? she wondered. Did he tire of people too? Was all this pleasure only a temporary dream, to be shattered as soon as her usefulness to Huntley had been expended? Was she the victim of a piece of wicked deception, as Negara insisted she was?

The evening had been something of an eye-opener for Claudia. Quite apart from its apparent rebuttal of Negara's accusation was Huntley's totally unexpected behavior on the beach. He seemed to shed his hotel manager's skin as easily as a suit of clothes, becoming a totally different person, carefree, chatting with the natives, laughing, and splashing through the waves.

Claudia's head began to spin with confusion, both over Huntley himself and over her own feelings for him. Even if he was simply playing her along for his own purposes, she decided as she drifted into sleep, it would be beyond her strength of will to walk out on him voluntarily now.

CHAPTER FIVE

Claudia made her way to the hotel kitchens next morning to find Monsieur Rekans, the head chef. By noon she would have to know all she needed to know about Indonesian cooking. She hoped M. Rekans would be a cooperative teacher.

Dodging a small army of junior cooks and kitchen boys, sniffing appreciatively at steaming caldrons as they stirred, she passed huge industrial dishwashers and what seemed like miles of stainless steel counter space before reaching the head chef's office behind a glass partition. The man sat with his back to her, his feet on the desk beside his round white chef's hat. He was reading a newspaper.

"Monsieur Rekans . . ." she began, and he whipped round, swinging his feet to the ground and his hat onto his head, all in one movement. The newspaper fell to the floor and lay there ignored.

"Ah, *nyonya*, I was expecting you," he said in an accent more reminiscent of France than the Far East. "*Monsieur le directeur* said you would be coming. I told him that I was really too busy, but he insisted that I attend to you personally." He stood up and shrugged his shoulders in a gesture of inevitability. "Ah, well, the guests' lunch it will suffer, but I have doubt that they will notice the difference. Now, *nyonya*, am I to understand that you wish to learn in an hour

79

or so about Indonesian cooking—that which it has taken me twenty years to acquire?"

Claudia gave him a humble smile. "Just the very basic rudiments, Monsieur Rekans, so that I can fool the hotel guests that I know something about what they are eating. Just tell me something about the typical Balinese dishes."

Rekans clapped a hand to his forehead. "Balinese dishes! There is no such, except perhaps *ikan masak Bali*, which is fish cooked with tamarind pulp, and not very good-tasting to a Javanese like myself. No, no, *nyonya*, here in our dining room we serve only the best Indonesian cuisine, and that of course is from Java."

"Oh," said Claudia, "I see."

"In our restaurant here at Bali Breezes," Rekans went on, "I make the food a little more palatable to Western tongue just as I used to in Amsterdam. Spices spattering in the cooking pan are the essence of our dishes . . ."

"Of course," Claudia cut in. "These islands were called the Spice Islands when the Dutch first conquered them."

"Precisely. Now the most important spice is the hot chili, both the longer one, the *cabe,* and the small green one, the *lombok,* named after the island to the east of Bali. But we also use very much of coriander; cumin; *serai,* or lemon grass; garlic; tumeric; *terasi;* ginger; basil; limes; *lengkuas . . .*"

Claudia produced the clipboard and pencil that she always carried with her, and scribbled down the names she could remember from Rekans' list.

"You know, I think," said the chef, "you will find that nine out of ten of the guests will order *rijsttafel,* which is the Dutch for rice table. So, if you learn by heart the eleven dishes that we serve as our *rijsttafel,* you will be able enough to impress the people with your knowledge. Here, I will show you each dish so that you will remember it at the table, and you will write down its name. How is that?"

"Fine," agreed Claudia, and they set out on a tour of the kitchen, Monsieur Rekans leading her from a steaming bowl of chicken soup, which Claudia duly recorded as *soto madura*, to beef noodles or *semin sapi*, to a *sambal* of liver with vegetable sauce. She was shown beef brains, called *gulai kambing, nasi goreng*, spicy fried rice, and the most popular of all Indonesian dishes, *satay*, which are small wooden skewers of chicken, beef, or pork ready to be dipped into a peanut butter sauce before eating. Shrimp, palm salad, and various fruits completed the *rijsttafel*.

"You're right," said Claudia. "If I rattle off all those names at dinner with the Germans, they'll think I know all about Indonesian food. I just hope they all order *rijsttafel*."

"You could always suggest it to them," said Rekans.

"If they ask for my recommendation. Personally, I think it's more likely that they'll want something typically Balinese."

Rekans stuck his nose in the air. "Then send them to the café in the village along the beach—the one where the old lady makes the *soto* that the *directeur* like so much, the one he took you to last night, or so my spies inform me."

Claudia was thunderstruck. "You know he took me out last night?"

"One of the girls who scrubs my floor lives there. She told me this morning that Monsieur Fox was there with a pretty blond girl with a broad smile of very white teeth. So when you come to my kitchen today I add the two and the two."

I wonder if he knew that we would be seen by that girl, mused Claudia. "Is she a blabbermouth?"

"I beg your pardon, *nyonya*, what is that?"

"A blabbermouth. Someone who will tell everybody in the hotel that we were out together."

"No, that girl is not of that kind. She mentioned it to me because I have told her to report it whenever the *directeur* goes there. It is important that I know what he eats outside the hotel. Although I must keep the guests satisfied with my cuisine, it is to Monsieur Fox that I owe my job. If he happens to like the old lady's *soto*," Rekans shrugged resignedly, "then I would be foolish not to follow the same recipe."

"So you think the girl won't tell anybody else?"

"Don't worry, *nyonya*. I know she will not. The secret of your romance is safe with me, you can be assured."

"There is no romance, I promise you. He just wanted to show me where the hotel might expand. That was all," said Claudia earnestly. "I'm relieved about the girl. You see, I was worried. . . ."

"No need," said Rekans. "But now you must learn all the dishes of the *rijsttafel*, if you wish to please *monsieur le directeur*, as I'm sure you do." He gave a conspiratorial wink and a final squeeze to her elbow. "And later, perhaps, if you wish to know about some special dish, you can come and consult with me again. Now I am too busy to attend further to you. Good-bye, *nyonya*."

He left her then and strode back to his cubicle. Before leaving the kitchen, Claudia could see him settled back with his feet on the desk, again absorbed in his newspaper.

That afternoon she settled down in her room with Huntley Fox's book on Bali, and tried to memorize as much as possible. The next morning she paid another visit to the museum and found that her homework had familiarized her with many more of the displays. Later, her driver took her up to the village of Mas to see an exhibition of woodcarving. So passed her three days of indoctrination as a tour guide and hostess; she only hoped she had reached the standard that the manager demanded of her.

During all that time she kept well out of the way of Anton, not wanting to be diverted from her task. She never saw Negara awake, because the dancer was still fast asleep by the time she left their room in the morning—on those occasions when Negara came back to the room at all at night. Claudia didn't cross paths with Huntley either, but on the fourth morning, she received a message from his secretary to present herself at his office at seventeen minutes past ten exactly.

She arrived a little ahead of the appointed time, and let Eleanor Davis know that she was waiting. At 10:17 on the dot, Huntley Fox showed the assistant manager out of his office, and beckoned to Claudia to come in. In his uniform of dark striped pants and black alpaca jacket, his glasses securely in place and a severe set to his mouth, he bore little resemblance to the man who had escorted her along the beach three nights ago.

"Come in, Claudia," he said brusquely. "I can spare you exactly six minutes this morning. But first I must let you know that the German party has been delayed, and won't be arriving until late this evening. They'll be too tired for any social activity, and will probably go straight to bed. I want you to meet them here in my office at ten o'clock tomorrow morning, prepared to take the ladies on their first excursion. All right?"

"Fine," said Claudia. "That gives me another day to bone up on the local color."

"Yes, you should have that list of mine fully completed by this evening." He stared at her for an uncomfortable moment, and then strolled across the room, rubbing his chin, talking over his shoulder. "Let me try you with a few simple questions. First, which is the holiest shrine in Bali?"

"Besakih, halfway up the side of Mount Agung, the volcano. Every pious Balinese has to make a pilgrimage there once in his lifetime."

"Right. What happened to those who were there in March 1963?"

"They were buried by molten lava from the eruption of Mount Agung."

"They were indeed. They made no attempt to escape. They accepted their fate as the will of God, all two thousand of them."

"When are you going to fly me up there in your helicopter?" asked Claudia, trying to bring the conversation around to a more personal level.

He brushed her reminder aside. "I've no idea. Now, here's another question. Why are some Balinese villages infested with rats?"

"Because their religion won't let them kill any living thing except for food."

"Quite right." He nodded gravely, facing the window. "How is it, then, that a village can rid itself of the pests?"

"I . . . I don't know. Is there a way?"

He turned to face her, speaking slowly, didactically. "The Balinese religion is Hinduism, elaborated of course, but basically Hinduism, as you know. But the government of Indonesia is officially Muslim, which has no such law against the slaughter of animals. So the government supplies the rat poison and a Balinese Hindu who puts it down is at that moment a Muslim government agent, and therefore not going against his own faith. Nice rationalization, isn't it?"

Claudia had been only half-listening to what he was saying. All through his dissertation, she had been wondering how to bring up the matter of them having been seen together on the beach. "Talking of rationalization," she said slowly, "and for that matter talking of poison, do you know that at least two members of the staff of this hotel already have been discussing the fact that you and I went out along the beach together last night?"

He seemed taken aback. "That's impossible. We sneaked out the back way."

"No staff actually saw us going or coming, as far as I know, unless you deliberately planned for us to pass a spot where somebody would see us without us seeing them." Claudia felt her mouth tightening as she spoke.

"What on earth are you talking about? You saw me take every precaution for us not to be seen."

"You certainly appeared to," Claudia admitted. "But are you sure that wasn't just for my benefit? Are you quite sure you don't want to start some rumors about us?"

"Of course not! That's the last thing I want. How could I possibly maintain the respect of the hotel staff if they thought that I was . . . was . . ."

"Interested in one of your female employees?"

"Exactly. It would lead to an untenable situation."

"And you don't think that any such stories are going the rounds at the moment?"

Huntley Fox opened his eyes wide, and for the first time Claudia saw him look discomfited. "Of course there can't possibly be any such stories," he said. "Or, if there are, they must be schoolgirl fabrications that nobody would bother to listen to. There are certainly no grounds for anything else."

"Of course," said Claudia, satisfied. Huntley might be harsh, but he had no guile. Negara's accusation was quite unfounded. If he was really so naive as to think that his feelings for Negara didn't show, he wouldn't have the cunning—nor the motive—to use Claudia as a decoy.

"That's enough of that subject." Huntley consulted his watch. "Just time for one more question. Tell me, Claudia, how does a Balinese react if he is annoyed with you?"

"He just gets angry with you, I guess."

"No, that's just what he doesn't do. It's considered very bad form to show anger. He plots to steal from you instead. Thievery for revenge is very common in Bali. And if you want back what he has stolen from you, you are expected to go and buy it back, even if you only pay a small price for it. Then you and the other person can become friends again."

"That *is* strange," said Claudia, "But suppose . . ."

"No time for more now," he cut her off. "Your six minutes are up. Tomorrow at ten, don't forget. Shut the door on your way out." He sat down abruptly at his desk, pushing back the stray lock of hair from his forehead. He didn't look up from his papers as she walked to the door and let herself out, softly closing it behind her.

Afraid of being alone with Huntley when he was in a mood to work, Claudia timed her arrival at his office for exactly ten the next morning. That way they wouldn't have to stand around together waiting for the German guests to arrive unless the guests were late, and Claudia knew from the experience of her family that punctuality is a German virtue.

But she didn't expect the honored group of seven to be already there when she arrived, with Eleanor Davis trying to fill in as hostess. The secretary gave her a look of relief as she came in, and darted back to her cubbyhole outside the office.

"Ah, there you are, Claudia," the manager snapped under his breath. Then, as all eyes turned toward her, he said to the three men, "Allow me to introduce Miss Claudia Bauer of my staff. She speaks fluent German, and will be able to communicate effectively with your wives, and your daughter, Herr Steiner, when she escorts them on the sight-seeing trips we have arranged for the ladies around the island."

Herr Steiner, a tall, military-looking man with wavy, graying hair and a clipped mustache, inclined his head slightly and took Claudia's hand to raise it an inch or two toward his face. "*Gnädiges Fräulein,*" he greeted her. "*Ich küsse die Hände.*"

How like the Germans, thought Claudia, to say they kiss your hand without coming anywhere near it, while the Latin races pour soulful kisses onto a girl's hand but don't talk about it.

She glanced around the room, acknowledging the introduction of the rest of the party as Huntley reeled off their names like a burst of machine-gun fire. The thin, severe-looking woman with a bun at the back of her head must be Herr Steiner's wife, she decided, and the well-built, blond girl of eighteen was their daughter. Then there was Herr Blum, short, nervously chain-smoking, with a bald head except for some straggly hair dangling over his collar at the back; he looked the henpecked type, so presumably the bubbling, tubby lady in a bright floral print was Frau Blum. That left the Hauptmanns, he an earnest, confident businessman with a paunch and darting eyes determined not to miss anything, and she a quiet, distant, gray-haired lady with a sour expression. She's going to complain about everything as we go round the island, thought Claudia. I must be careful with her.

The ebullient lady in the print dress, who had curly

fair hair and very red lipstick, came over to seize Claudia's hand and pat it appreciatively. *"So!"* she smiled, *"Du bist deutsch, Fräulein?"*

"No, I'm not a German citizen," Claudia answered her in her own language. "I'm as American as Mr. Fox—I mean Huntley—here, but my parents were German and we often speak it at home. I hope you can understand my accent, Frau Blum."

The lady's laughing assertion that she could understand Claudia easily was drowned by a scathing hiss from Huntley Fox as he pulled her aside. "Claudia! That isn't Frau Blum, it's Frau Steiner, the mother of Hilda here. Frau Blum is the lady with the bun. That's a bad start, getting their names mixed up. You'll have to do better than that!"

"I'm sorry," Claudia whispered back, feeling wretched for her mistake. She was allowed no time to dwell on it because Frau Steiner, apparently unaware that Claudia had addressed her wrongly, was exuberantly extolling the virtues of Bali. She ended by asking Claudia where she was going to take them that day.

"Well, I thought we'd look in at the Denpasar market first," she said, "and then go on to the batik factory. We'll have lunch at an air-conditioned restaurant in the city, and then drive inland a few miles to a village called Mas, where the best woodcarvers are. And we can visit the artists at Ubud. Unless, of course, you'd rather come back to the hotel for a siesta or a swim."

"Oh, no!" said Frau Steiner. "We mustn't waste a moment of our time in this fascinating island. We must see all we can."

"I get tired easily," asserted Frau Hauptmann in a tone that seemed to accuse Claudia of having tired her out already.

"I want to spend as much time as I can swimming,"

said Hilda, thus earning a rebuke from her mother, who insisted that Hilda was here for her education as much as for her lazy pleasures.

Frau Blum, obviously assuming a familiar role as the settler of arguments, resolved this one by announcing that she would make the decision as to whether to continue the tour after lunch or not when the time came. In the meanwhile, would Fräulein Claudia kindly lead the way to their car so that they could commence the day's activities. The men, Frau Blum added, would not be accompanying them, as there would be little to interest them in either the market, the batik factory, or the woodcarvers. Nobody disputed these remarks; the party had certainly already learned not to argue with Frau Blum. Thank goodness for her, thought Claudia. She is going to save me from a lot of difficult mediation as the days go by.

The morning went strictly according to plan. Frau Steiner enthused over the marvelous assortment of native fruits at the market, while Frau Hauptmann complained about the smell of bad drains, and Hilda just looked bored. Everyone, however, enjoyed the batik factory, and they bought so many skirts and lengths of top-quality material that Mr. Mutiara was delighted, and whispered to Claudia that he would be sending her a small token of his gratitude for bringing such excellent customers to his shop.

A cooling lunch at the Hotel Indonesia was followed by the pronouncement by Frau Blum that it was still early, and that they all still had enough energy to drive to Mas to visit the woodcarvers, but that would be all. Nobody raised any objection to this plan, so the car drew up outside the open-air woodcarving school in the early afternoon. For half an hour they watched the pupils at work under the direction of their professor, and then each member of the party purchased a small carving—offered to them at a bargain forty percent below the regular price—except Frau Steiner, who bought three pieces, being unable to choose between them.

By three o'clock they had arrived safely back at the Bali Breezes and gone their separate ways. When they had all disappeared, Claudia thanked the driver, and instructed him to stand by at nine o'clock the next morning. Then she made her way up to the manager's office to report their return, and to seek instructions for her next duties.

Eleanor Davis consulted the timetable of arrangements that Huntley Fox had dictated to her for the entertainment of the German guests. It appeared that he and Claudia were to meet them in a small private lounge on the main floor for predinner cocktails at seven that evening before going into dinner in the main restaurant.

Claudia decided that this program merited a sophisticated new dress—hadn't Huntley told her to get some new clothes?—so she cruised through the boutiques near the hotel entrance, looking for something suitable. Eventually she found a simple knee-length dress with a shirred top made of the crispest gingham check. She bought some high-heeled sandals to go with it.

Throughout the cocktail party and the dinner that followed it, most of the conversation was conducted in German for the benefit of the ladies. Claudia glued herself to Huntley's side and translated for him any remarks that she felt might interest him. As the evening progressed, Frau Steiner fell into a routine of telling somewhat feeble jokes; Claudia did her best to pass on to her employer a version of these absurdities. He usually just smiled wanly at Frau Steiner when Claudia had finished.

Claudia was most gratified that all three of the wives went out of their way to tell Huntley Fox how well their conductor had looked after them; even Hilda vaguely echoed their comments. At this, the manager turned his inscrutable eyes on Claudia and muttered some general words of approval. From him, this was praise indeed.

As chef Rekans had predicted, all the guests ordered *rijsttafel,* and in due course the eleven dishes that Claudia had memorized were laid before them. The ladies turned eagerly to her for an explanation of what they contained. She recited the local name and ingredients of each one without error. The men too listened hungrily until she had finished. At the mention of the beef brains, Frau Hauptmann made a noise signifying distaste, a signal ignored by the others.

Conversation about the food burst into a babble as each dish circulated the table, until all the diners were satisfied that they hadn't missed anything. Silence fell as they simultaneously attacked their choices.

Taking advantage of the quiet, broken only by steady munching, Huntley Fox announced that tomorrow, while the ladies were on another excursion with Claudia, he would take the gentlemen up in his helicopter to the summit of Mount Agung, the highest of the three volcanoes in Bali. Mount Batur, nearby, was active at the moment and dangerous to visit, but Agung was safe, and he hoped the men would appreciate the trip. All three nodded their assent.

Claudia then told the legend that Bali was a completely flat island when all Indonesia was of Hindu faith, but when the other islands converted to Islam and only the Balinese remained Hindu, the Hindu gods created these three great mountains so that they would have suitably elevated places for immortal gods to live. Everyone grunted their interest in the story, and when Claudia gave Huntley a brief translation in English, he expressed his approval too.

At that moment Herr Hauptmann nudged Frau Steiner, who was sitting next to him, and pointed at the dish of chicken *satay* skewers, asking her to pass it to him for a second helping. That reminded Claudia to tell the assembled company that the Balinese never point with the index finger—it is in fact a gesture of irreverence—but always use the thumb instead. "As though they were hitchhiking," she added in explanation.

Even Hilda, who had so far spent most of the evening gazing around the room, expressed amusement at this snippet of information. Herr Steiner, in his usual clipped, formal mode of speech, said that Claudia must have lived for a long time among the Balinese to know so much of their folklore. But Claudia just laughed and said that her knowledge was nothing compared to the manager's, who had been studying it for years. "Tell them some other interesting example, Huntley," she encouraged him, trying to put on the air of easy familiarity he had suggested.

"Well, there's the legend about the fearful eruption of Mount Agung in 1963," he said, with Claudia translating. "The story goes that the holy mountain did it as an act of retribution, its death-dealing lava purposefully tracking down and smothering every man who had ever cut down trees from its sides, taken sulfur from its crater, or even picked the fruit that grows at its base. It was this attitude of inevitability that kept official relief work to a mere token. Thousands were simply left to starve."

"That's a real disaster," said Herr Blum, and the somber note that Huntley's remarks had introduced cast a slight pall over the party. Soon afterward, when everybody had finished eating, he suggested that they all move upstairs to the nightclub on the top floor for music and dancing.

The headwaiter in the rooftop room hurriedly arranged for three tables to be pushed together in a select position opposite the dance floor, and everyone took a seat. Claudia noted that the husbands and wives chose to sit together, as if in self-protection against the slightly lascivious atmosphere of the low lights and intimate music. Claudia again placed herself beside Huntley, rationalizing that this was her dutiful position as a translator.

The headwaiter must have got wind of the presence of Germans in the manager's party, because the band suddenly broke into a medley of tunes in typical oom-pah-pah style. Herr Steiner at once asked Claudia to dance; he whisked her around in his own variety of a polka step until he began panting severely, and willingly accepted her suggestion that they sit down.

Claudia had hardly settled herself when Anton Reinholtz appeared suddenly behind her chair and asked her for a dance. Hearing a quick intake of breath from Huntley beside her, Claudia excused herself on the grounds of being on duty, but, thinking in a flash, introduced Anton to Hilda Steiner.

"*Er ist auch deutsch,*" Claudia told Hilda, at which she shrugged in simulated boredom.

Hilda's apparent disinterest must have fired the requisite spark in Anton, because he immediately took his cue and laid a hand on her shoulder from behind. "*Willst du tanzen?*" he asked her in his smoothest tone.

"Okay," Hilda replied in the universal language of the casual, and they moved onto the floor. After the dance was over, she joined the group of young people sitting with Anton on the other side of the room.

The Hauptmanns got up to dance now, and Claudia heard Huntley inquiring in a diffident voice if she would like to try the floor as well. "But I'm afraid I can't dance the energetic German style. You'll excuse me if I ask the band to switch to something more to my taste."

"If you like," she replied, wondering if he would request rock or jazz.

He spoke to the bandleader and within moments the combo had wound up the brassy drinking song they had been pounding out, and slid into an old-fashioned slow number from the forties. Huntley's arm went firmly around her waist and pressed her against him as he began to glide in perfect rhythm across the floor. The sensation started an unexpected quickening of her pulse, but she refused to bother about this and laid her cheek happily against his coat lapel.

When they had circled the floor twice in this fashion and she had noticed a few curious eyes focused on them, she suddenly remembered Negara's warning. Was Huntley dancing close and seductively with her simply to parade her in front of other members of the hotel staff? Was his apparent solicitude artificial, a ploy to distract gossipers from his relationship to Negara herself? In sudden dismay, she stiffened up, and drew back from him.

He looked down at her quizzically as they continued to sway to the beat of the music. "Is anything the matter?" he asked.

"Well," she replied, "isn't this a bit public for the manager and one of his newest staff members to be quite so . . . schmaltzy?"

"I suppose you're right," he said. "We've been having such a pleasant evening that I forgot about the wagging tongues." Soon afterward the music came to an end and he led her quickly back to the table.

Not much later, the Hauptmanns announced that they were tired and going to bed. Frau Blum then said that all the ladies who were going off again with Claudia tomorrow, as well as Claudia herself, should get a good rest if they were going to be fit for the excursion. The Steiners finished their drinks and got up; Claudia was dispatched to fetch a mildly protesting Hilda from Anton's table; and Huntley shepherded the whole party toward the elevators.

Claudia was the only one to get off at the eighth floor. "*Gute Nacht,*" she bade them all, and they chorused their thanks.

"Good night, Claudia," said Huntley Fox, flashing her one of his rare but devastating smiles. "I'm sure we're all looking forward to more of your pleasant company tomorrow."

"I won't see you gentlemen until the evening." Claudia gave them an all-embracing smile back. "But if you ladies would like to meet me in the lobby at nine . . ."

"We'll be there, not a minute later," said Frau Blum in her usual role as spokesman, just as the elevator door closed in her face.

The next morning Frau Blum's promise of punctuality extended even to Hilda Steiner, as the four female Germans were already grouped by the front entrance when Claudia appeared. The ladies were in sleeveless cotton dresses and Hilda in T-shirt and jeans, and they found it hard to believe Claudia when she strongly recommended that each of them go and fetch a warm sweater, since the wind at the highest point of their proposed tour, the village of Kintamani, was decidedly chilly at an altitude of five thousand feet.

For the first hour, the car lurched, bounced, and swerved up the northbound road through fairly heavy traffic connecting numerous small *kampong* villages, each huddled around its ornate brick temple in a forest clearing. The passengers rattled across narrow bridges of loose planks, below which sparkling water tumbled over rocks, the heavy scented air under the arcade of trees sometimes flashing with the blue and white of a kingfisher, scarlet at the bill.

Then, leaving the jungle below them, they began to climb a river valley, the tires throwing up dust and gravel at every corner. The river's course was no longer its natural one, for every square yard of hillside had been terraced and planted with emerald-green rice, the terraces climbing steeply, and irregularly. Balinese farmers had so skillfully diverted the river that a small branch of it flooded each terrace before cascading down a manmade channel to irrigate those further down. They stopped for a moment to admire the unique beauty of Bali—bank upon bank of vivid green, the white gush of water, and the flawless blue sky above.

At the top, huddled in their sweaters at the window of Kintamani's solitary restaurant, they gazed at the conical peak of Mount Batur, directly across from them beyond a valley of forbidding gray lava, cold and solid. The lava inhibited the growth of plant life right up to its flattened crater, from which innocent little puffs of white smoke emerged every few minutes, soon to drift away and dissipate into the azure sky.

To their right lay the icy stillness of Lake Batur, and beyond it, towering up to over ten thousand feet, rose the holy peak of Mount Agung, dormant now but still a fearful reminder of previous divine wrath. As Claudia gazed at it, a speck in the sky appeared from the south, quickly assuming the ungainly shape of a helicopter. Tip-tilted, it circled over Kintamani with its rotor pulsating loudly, and then sped away to remain poised for a moment over Mount Agung's crater.

Gingerly it came down, to settle daintily as a butterfly on the mountain's highest point.

Straining her eyes, Claudia could just make out four human beings leaving the helicopter to remain silhouetted against the brilliant sky for a moment before vanishing from view. A pang of jealousy hit her. Hadn't Huntley promised he would try out the jaunt to Mount Agung on her before offering it to any more hotel guests? It was most unfair of him not to have taken her first.

The sudden feeling of dissatisfaction with her job made her decide to put into action her plan to arrange for the Germans to see Penebel dance the *ramayana* ballet. In his capacity as host to the party, Huntley could scarcely refuse to come too. Claudia couldn't wait to see the expression on Huntley's face as he watched Penebel's graceful movements. Surely he would be able to see how much better she was than Negara, in spite of his personal bias toward the latter.

Claudia addressed the assembled ladies, "On our way back to the hotel we could stop in a little village called Bedulu—that is, if you'd like to. It has the best dancing school in Bali, and we might be able to watch the dancers practicing."

Frau Steiner was ecstatic. "Oh, that would be just perfect."

"Will it take long to go by this place Bedulu?" asked Frau Hauptmann doubtfully. "I don't want to arrive back at the hotel completely exhausted."

"Yes, we will go by Bedulu," stated Frau Blum. "No visit to Bali would be complete without seeing a dancing school. We will leave in five minutes."

Compliance with Frau Blum's orders was an accepted fact among the group, and very shortly they were heading back down the twisting road, leaving the cold barren region of the volcanoes to the hardy inhabitants of Kintamani and their merciless gods.

CHAPTER SIX

Down in the steaming jungle the driver, who was delighted with the opportunity to again visit his cousin Tabanan at Bedulu, swung the car into a sharp turn and headed into the village.

The German ladies were disappointed to find that the dancers were not practicing that afternoon, but Tabanan was in his house and invited the whole party inside. Claudia whispered to her flock to watch carefully what she did when entering, so that they would know the custom that must be followed by a visitor to a Balinese home.

Leading the way through Tabanan's front door under the glazed eyes of its guardian Rangda, Claudia approached her host with her knees and body slightly bent in an attitude of humility. In her right hand she held a matchbox, offering it as a gift to Tabanan, her left hand grasping her right elbow in the traditional fashion. "*Selamat datang*," she said in greeting.

"*Terina kasih*—thank you, my dear Claudia," Tabanan replied, accepting the small gift. "You are very quickly becoming one of us. I am honored by your visit. Are these your friends from the hotel whom you were telling me about? The ones who wish to see our dance?"

"These are the ladies," said Claudia, introducing the Germans. "But I am hoping their husbands will also come, and the hotel manager as well." She turned to the ladies, who were examining the dark, barely furnished room, Frau Steiner and Frau Blum showing interest, Frau Hauptmann and Hilda poorly disguised distaste. "How would you like to drive up here with the gentlemen tomorrow evening and watch a dance performance in real native surroundings?" she asked. "You can see Balinese dancing at the hotel, but it's not as authentic, and the chief dancer here is much better, I promise you."

The three women assented with enthusiasm. Tabanan hurried off to consult the *bailan*, the witch doctor, who said the performance tomorrow would be auspicious, provided the guests arrived with *bantan*, or offerings of food to present to the *pemankah*, curator of the temple. Arrangements were made for the following evening. Penebel would dance the leading role.

But Claudia had underestimated the manager's powers of resistance, even against Frau Blum's gift of persuasion. When the group returned to the hotel, the three husbands capitulated immediately with barely a word of protest when told that they would be accompanying their wives to Bedulu. The announcement was made at an informal gathering in Huntley's office that evening.

"I hope you'll be coming too," Claudia cooed to him, out of earshot of the others. "You'll love the new little dancer, Penebel."

"It's too late to do anything about it now, Claudia," he answered sternly. "But I never said you were to make arrangements for the evening entertainment of the guests. That is strictly my business."

"But they're all so keen to go . . ."

"The ladies are, I agree. That's why I'm not too mad about your arranging it. But don't do it again." He turned to see the Germans preparing to leave.

"We are all tired tonight," said Herr Steiner, coming over to where Huntley and Claudia were standing. "So I hope you will excuse us if we retire to bed early. Thank you again, Herr Fox, for an unforgettable journey to Mount Agung. And you, Claudia, for the equally delightful day you provided for our families." He clicked his heels gently, inclined his head toward her, and ushered the party out of the office toward the elevators.

"I feel like a snack before getting back to work," said Huntley. "Do you want to come down to the coffee shop with me?"

Claudia hesitated, mindful of Negara's warning. "Do you think it's good for us to be seen together in public?"

"That's why I suggested the coffee shop. It's always deserted at this time of night."

"All right, then," Claudia said. "I could use a bite to eat."

The Kopi Shop, as the sign in Indonesian designated, lay at the end of a covered walk away from the main building of the hotel. As Huntley and Claudia made their way along this colonnade, a figure in purple silk pajamas limped toward them, supported by a cane. It was Negara. Huntley tensed visibly, and Negara gave Claudia a knowing look along with her smile of greeting.

"Negara!" Claudia cried. "What have you done to yourself?"

"Sprained my ankle," the dancer replied, holding up a swollen foot encased in a heavy bandage.

"How did you do it, Negara?" asked Huntley Fox solicitously.

"Well, I'm sure you wouldn't want to hear about the exact circumstances"—Negara's eyes flashed mischievously—"but I found myself in the position of having to jump from a bed onto the floor, and I landed on the side of my foot. That wasn't meant to be part of the position."

"Whose bed?" demanded Huntley.

"Now, now," Negara teased him. "That would be my business, wouldn't it."

The manager sucked in a breath through clenched teeth, but kept silent for a moment. Then, composing himself, he said, "Does this mean you won't be able to dance on Saturday? Or will it be better by then?"

"No, I'm afraid not. The doctor says two weeks."

"That's terrible. What's on the program for Saturday?"

"The *barong* and *kris* dance. You'll have to find someone else to take the part of the *dewi*. It involves a lot of steps."

"Dammit!" the manager exploded. "Quite apart from all the other guests, I particularly wanted our German group to see you, Negara."

"I don't give a damn what you wanted, Huntley!" Negara burst in angrily. "I'm sure that your uncle, when he arrives, will be just as happy to have me in the audience with him as up on the stage."

Huntley Fox turned away in disgust, seizing hold of Claudia's elbow. "Come on, Claudia. Come to the coffee shop."

As he started striding away from Negara, almost pushing Claudia ahead of him, the dancer called after them, "You should have graduated beyond the coffee shop by now, Claudia. Keep trying, dear. Maybe you'll make it to the bar next. But can't you see it's not for real?"

"What did she mean by that?" snapped Huntley as they sped along.

"I really don't know," said Claudia. "I thought you might."

They sat in silence opposite each other in a booth, munching their sandwiches and sipping strong Javanese coffee.

Finally Claudia broke the invisible barrier between them. "You didn't say whether you were coming with us to Bedulu tomorrow night. I wish you would. I know the Germans would appreciate it."

"No, I've no intention of going. It'll give me a chance to catch up on some work. Besides, we have a much better dance troupe here in the hotel."

"But for two weeks your star is going to be out of action."

"I know, dammit!" He glared across the table. "I hope one of the other girls knows the part of the *dewi*, but I very much doubt it."

"It's a big part," said Claudia, and then added, seizing the opportunity boldly, "but I'm certain Penebel knows it. The *barong* and *kris* is one of the most popular of all the dances. Come with us tomorrow evening, Huntley, please do! I know that once you've seen Penebel dance, you'll agree that she could replace Negara until her ankle's better."

Huntley continued to look surly. He pushed back the stray lock of hair that flopped across his forehead, and patted it in place. "I'm not sure I want some little country girl up in front of all the rich and sophisticated hotel guests. They're used to professionals on stage."

"But the Germans are rich and sophisticated, and *they* want to see Penebel," she argued.

"That's different. It's sort of like slumming to them. Anyway, they're only going because Frau Blum didn't give them the chance to refuse."

Claudia laughed. "I can't deny that. She's quite the gorgon, isn't she. But I'll bet they won't be disappointed. Come on, Huntley, come and see Penebel for yourself. If you don't think she's up to it, you don't have to ask her down here for Saturday."

"That's true," Huntley grudgingly agreed. "All right, I'll come. I suppose I should explore all the possibilities before canceling the show for the next two weeks. I'm sure none of our other girls could fill in."

"Great!" Claudia smiled at him. "Besides, I'll enjoy your company."

"That's another reason for me to come," he smiled back at her, and the moment became suddenly intimate.

Because of the excitement and exertion of going up to Bedulu the next evening, Frau Blum had decreed that the ladies' sight-seeing tour would be confined to a trip to the Denpasar Museum in the morning. The afternoon would be a rest period. As usual, nobody argued with this decision.

Claudia got through the visit to the museum with more ease than she had hoped. Frau Steiner showed surprising interest in the Seven Heavenly Seers, and they were all quite horrified at the model of the tooth-pulling ceremony. Claudia's memorized explanations appeared to satisfy them, except for Hilda, who gave up all pretense at involvement and waited for them on the steps outside. They were back in the hotel soon after eleven.

Remembering that they were expected to arrive at Bedulu bearing some sort of offerings to present to the *pemankah* in order to assure the auspiciousness of tonight's dance, Claudia went to the kitchen to enlist Rekans's aid in preparing something suitable.

"It is of course a nonsense," he said. "Proper festivals include symbolic foods that don't provide much nour-

103

ishment—things such as thin panes of rice paste painted with the portrait of a goddess and sticky sweets of licorice—but what the head men of Bedulu want from you is a bribe in the form of some of the best cooking available in Bali—mine!"

"I'm sure you're right," laughed Claudia. "Put together as much as you can spare, please, Monsieur Rekans. We want them to put on a specially good performance tonight."

"For you, I will do it, *nyonya*," he replied, pushing his chef's hat forward over his eyes at a jaunty angle. "For you and for the *directeur*, to whom, of course, you have no romantic attachment." He dug his elbow into her side and smiled comically.

"If you want to have your little game, you can," said Claudia. "But there's no truth in what you're saying. Just get together a good feast for the village."

"I will," grinned Rekans. "I want your evening to be perfect."

The group of seven Germans, Huntley Fox, and Claudia were driven up to Bedulu. The whole village was waiting when they pulled up in the dusty compound that served as the auditorium. On the right, a single row of mismatched chairs stiffly faced the stage, beyond which the shadows of the brick temple and surrounding undergrowth were just discernible in the pale moonlight. A string of naked bulbs suspended from the trees around the compound gave enough illumination for the visitors' greeting ceremony.

Tabanan came forward, bowing with each step, his battered straw hat in hand. Claudia introduced him to Huntley Fox and then to each of the German men; he smiled a general welcome to the ladies, which only Frau Steiner acknowledged. Then he indicated the *bailan,* a seedy-looking old man with a concave chest and very thin brown arms, and the *pemankah,* a tall, much younger fellow in a splendid helmet of red and gold, with wings at each side and a curved spike at the back. He stood proudly, impassive as a guardsman on parade.

Huntley knew the routine formality. Signaling his driver to bring forward the great hamper of food that Rekans had prepared, he personally unpacked it in front of the *pemankah.* The holy man did his best to maintain his dignity, in spite of the rare succulence of each delicacy as it appeared. There were whole roast chickens, dishes of spicy rice, grilled fish in banana leaves, fruit of all kinds, and an assortment of nuts.

The crowd gathered eagerly around, gasping in amazement as each new offering was presented, the children barely restrained from reaching out to grab something. Two of the *pemankah*'s henchmen quickly packed all the food away again and carried it off into the night, followed by a fair-sized procession of those who had been invited to partake, together with a number of hopeful hangers-on.

The ceremony over, Tabanan led the visitors to their chairs. Huntley himself supervised the seating, placing Claudia in the middle of the row so as to be available to anyone for translation duties. He took a chair beside Tabanan, and Claudia noticed that they became quickly absorbed in earnest conversation.

For several minutes there was a good deal of scurrying about on the darkened stage, and then four men came running up with flaming, smoking torches at the same moment as the *gamelan* struck up the overture for the *ramayana* ballet. Half a dozen musicians worked feverishly over their floating metal xylophones and other percussion instruments, producing a harmonious, rhythmical sound. As always, it thrilled Claudia to hear it, and she leaned forward eagerly in her seat awaiting the dancers' entrance.

The initial performer was a young man in white tights and gloves under his *kamben polen,* a black-and-white checked skirt with ornamental belt and bright blue sash, his head covered by a grotesque bearded mask. The god he represented danced wildly with his companions to the ever-increasing tempo of the *gamelan;* then suddenly the music fell to a slow tinkle, the men on the stage went down on their knees, and Penebel appeared sinuously among them from out of the shadows.

In costume she was infinitely more impressive than she had been during the practice session Claudia had witnessed last week. Her green-and-gold strapless gown hugged her body from her breasts to her ankles, a crimson chiffon band trailing from her waist to the floor and an ornate gold headdress fitting closely above dangling earrings, while her own jet-black hair swept down her back to her thighs. She moved stealthily, her body weaving like a boneless snake. Nobody in the guest audience or in the crowd of squatting villagers on either side of them moved a muscle until she had come to the end of her first slow, seductive performance. Then, unable to control themselves, they burst into wild, spontaneous applause.

Claudia stole a glance at Huntley Fox. He was clapping like the rest and, catching her eye, he nodded and smiled at her. But his look revealed none of that the overwhelming fascination that he had shown when watching Negara dance.

While Penebel was resting during the next part of the ballet, and the white-bearded god held center stage, Claudia let her thoughts ramble to Huntley and Negara. How could such an intelligent, self-controlled man as he be so struck by her that he was able to overlook the kind of maddening insolence she threw at him last night when announcing her sprained ankle? How could he stand her taunting references to other men's beds? How could he still hope—indeed why would he ever want to hope—that she would become his, when she so blatantly affirmed that it was his uncle, Wilbur Fox, whom she has determined to snare into marriage? How could he be so blind and foolish?

Claudia found the situation rather sad. Although Huntley seemed to find her a satisfactory employee, it would be nice if he recognized her as a woman as well. Once or twice her hopes for a closer relationship had risen, but each time they had been dashed to the ground later when he had once more treated her with the cold efficiency of a computer.

At all events, she no longer had to worry about Negara's fanciful theory that she was being employed as a decoy to hide his infatuation for the dancer. His obviously sincere remark that there couldn't possibly be any romantic rumors going around about him made nonsense of that theory.

Daydreams of Huntley regarding her as truly feminine subconsciously induced her to smooth over her knees the exquisite batik dress that Mr. Mutiara had sent her and make minute adjustments to the way it clung tightly over her rounded breasts. As she did so, she turned to look at Huntley. To her horror she saw that his gaze was directed intensely upon her movements. She blushed to the roots of her hair, and turned quickly away, concentrating every nerve on the dance being enacted in front of her.

All the Germans gave the second half of the dance their rapt attention, and applauded loudly at the end. While Penebel and the other performers bowed graciously, Huntley turned to Tabanan beside him and spoke earnestly in Indonesian. The old man threw up his hands in delight and beckoned Penebel to come down from the stage to meet the hotel manager.

During the conversation in Indonesian that followed, Huntley remained calm and businesslike, but Tabanan seized his hand and shook it warmly, while Penebel's already round eyes grew wider and her lips parted in a happy smile. Claudia's impatience to know what was being said got the better of her at last and she pulled at Huntley's sleeve, a movement that caused him to whip round and shake her off.

"I . . . I'm sorry," she said. "I didn't mean to be rude, but I'm dying to know what you're talking about."

"Your idea was a good one," he acknowledged gravely. "I am making arrangements for Penebel to take Negara's place at the hotel until her leg is better."

"What are you offering?" asked Claudia.

"That Penebel receive half of Negara's regular salary, and that the Bedulu school receive an equal amount to compensate it for the loss of her for two weeks. Mr. Tabanan tells me that the school needs money badly for new costumes."

"That's great!" exclaimed Claudia. "And afterward, when Penebel comes back here to dance, I'm sure Mr. Fox will arrange regular visits to Bedulu by guests at the hotel. Everyone can see how much the Germans enjoyed it tonight."

Huntley's face clouded. "Don't put words into my mouth, Claudia," he said sternly. "With Negara available to my guests as entertainment, they would have no wish to travel up here to watch Penebel. She is, after all, only an amateur, although a good one, I agree."

Claudia bit her lip to prevent herself from pointing out that it was Penebel's authenticity that put her head and shoulders above a professional dancer like

Negara, to whom the Balinese grace did not come naturally.

Tabanan had his own reasons for not wanting Bedulu to be included as a regular feature on the hotel circuit. "Visits from time to time, like tonight, will be very welcome, but I think our dancers would become spoiled like those in Denpasar if they frequently had audiences of tourists. As the *tuan* says, we are amateurs—and would prefer to stay that way. Meanwhile, for Penebel it will be a great experience; yet I think that at the end of it she will be glad to return to Bedulu."

Tabanan translated this last remark so that Penebel could understand it, but Penebel made a face and shook her head vigorously. Tabanan laid a gnarled hand on her soft young shoulder and said wisely, "You will see, my dear, you will see."

Claudia traveled with Huntley Fox and the three Steiners for the trip back to Bali Breezes. The Germans were ecstatic in their praise of the performance they had just seen, but Huntley tried to dampen their enthusiasm. "I'm glad you enjoyed it," he said. "But you must appreciate that this is just a village school, and to compare their style to the regular dances we put on at the hotel is like comparing a school play to professional acting. That girl Penebel is not in the same league as our lead dancer, Negara. It is most unfortunate that she has injured her leg while you are here."

None so blind, thought Claudia, as those who will not see.

"That reminds me," said Herr Steiner to the manager. "Would you be able to accommodate my wife and daughter at the hotel for another week after I leave? I am compelled to go back to Düsseldorf to attend to business, I regret, but my family has asked to stay on. I have seldom seen them enjoy a holiday so much."

"I'm sure we can arrange it," Huntley replied. "I will see that Claudia continues to set up excursions of interest for them."

So he wants me to stay on, thought Claudia, suddenly gleeful. I wonder if it's just because he's prepared to do anything to satisfy these important Germans, or whether he wants me to stay for any more personal reason, and is using the Steiners' appreciation of my services as an excuse. At any rate, whoopee! I can't wait to see Penebel take over from Negara in the hotel dances.

What fun it would be if Negara also lost her position as Huntley's personal goddess! For that would open the door for somebody much more worthy to take over . . .

"Come upstairs for a snack before you go off to bed," Huntley told her after they had said good night to the Steiners in the hotel lobby. "I'd like to tell you about tomorrow's program. In the morning we'll all go to the Balinese Cultural Center, which is an institution I started in Denpasar last year."

As they came out of the elevator and walked past the row of deserted administrative offices, they heard laughter and voices coming from the open door of Huntley's own office.

"Somebody's in there," said Claudia, puzzled.

"Oh, no! Don't tell me he's come early," Huntley hissed between gritted teeth. "I didn't expect him till next week."

Lounging on the sofa, iced drinks in their hands, were Negara, looking gorgeous in a long clinging silk dress, which concealed the bandaged ankle, and a portly man with white hair and a mustache. He wore a travel-creased cream seersucker suit and a flamboyant tie, and struggled to his feet to greet Huntley by grasping his hand between both his own pudgy ones.

"Waal, Huntley my boy, it's good to see you again."

"Hullo, Uncle Wilbur," the manager responded without much emotion. "Did you have a good trip?"

"It's always a good trip to be coming back here," said Wilbur Fox, subsiding again onto the sofa and giving Negara's knee a playful slap. "And how's the season going? Your report for the last quarter quoted eighty-eight percent occupancy, which isn't bad, but I wasn't too happy about the profit margin. And from what I saw coming in, you're still employing those room boys. I told you last time I was here to chuck 'em out and take on girls as room maids instead—you could get 'em for half the salary you pay those boys. And they wouldn't sneak off with their tips the way those boys do."

"We've been into that before, Uncle," said Huntley sharply. "Those room boys are fathers of families and need the money for support. If I sack them now, our name in Bali . . ."

"To hell with our name in Bali," Wilbur cut in, his round cheeks taking on a slightly florid hue. "It's the bottom line I care about. My hotels aren't philanthropic enterprises, you know."

"Oh, Wilbur darling," said Negara petulantly, "don't argue with the poor boy as soon as you get here. You haven't said hello to Huntley's latest little friend. Wilbur Fox, Claudia . . . Claudia, I forget what your other name is, dear." She waved her champagne glass vaguely in Claudia's direction.

"Negara! You shouldn't introduce me like that," Claudia said. "You know perfectly well that I'm simply a member of the staff here . . ."

"Oh, yes, I know that," Negara grinned wickedly, "but as far as the rest of the hotel is concerned, including the manager, you're a very special member."

Wilbur Fox pushed himself back in the sofa and regarded Claudia quizzically, his head cocked to one side. "Negara explained your position to me," he said not unkindly. "I'm glad Huntley's found somebody, er, somebody to entertain his special guests. And himself of course."

Claudia flushed. "Mr. Fox, I'd like you to know that, in spite of any rumors to the contrary, my relationship with your nephew is purely a business one. Isn't it, Huntley?"

The manager didn't seem to have heard the conversation, and came out of some sort of reverie to say uncertainly, "Oh . . . oh, yes, of course, Claudia," before relapsing into silence again—a silence that he himself broke by addressing his uncle on the previous topic. "But you must understand that our reputation on the island as a good employer and an economic asset is important, Uncle. If these people ever came to think that we were exploiting them in any way . . ."

"You can't exploit people as far down the ladder as they are," Wilbur Fox came back. "There's only one way they can go and that's up. So any wages we pay them is better than they would have otherwise."

The argument made Claudia feel uncomfortable. She could see now why Huntley had dreaded his uncle's arrival. They obviously had quite different philosophies about running a business. She excused herself and went to bed, leaving the two men still sparring.

In her room, confusion and doubt returned. Why hadn't Huntley backed up more strongly her assertion that there was nothing personal between them? Did

Huntley want him to believe that there was? Wilbur obviously did still believe it. Did Huntley want the whole hotel to believe it, as Negara had suggested? Or was he vague about it simply because the matter of how to run the hotel was occupying his mind? She tried to persuade herself that that was the answer.

Yet if Wilbur was considering marriage to Negara, as the dancer had hinted, wouldn't he be more likely to propose to her if he thought that he wouldn't be treading on his nephew's toes in the process? It was one thing to argue about how the hotel should be run, but quite another to steal the manager's girl from under his nose. That could lead to an irreconcilable rift between them, something that Wilbur would hesitate to bring about. Having Wilbur think that Claudia was now Huntley's chief interest might help send Negara on her way back to the States with Wilbur—*that* was something devoutly to be hoped for, as it would soon rid Huntley of his infatuation for the dancer, and leave the field open to someone else. Even to Claudia herself. That is if she wanted it. . . .

All these disturbing thoughts made sleep impossible; Claudia had settled down at the dressing table to write a letter to her mother, when a gentle knock on her door caused her to put down her pen. Huntley stood outside in blue jeans and rope-soled sandals.

"How'd you like to come out fishing in one of the *jukungs* from the village?" he whispered conspiratorially. "Wilbur and Negara have taken over my suite, so I've no hope of getting to bed yet. It's a beautiful night, and I thought you might . . ."

In minutes she was in jeans and sandals herself and at the rudder of an outrigger canoe, guiding it through the surf. A red-and-yellow striped sail billowed above her in the gentle puff of wind; Huntley sat in the bow

113

attaching bait to his fishing line. A brilliant swath of moonlight cut through the ocean as far as the star-dappled horizon.

Then Huntley stood up, his tall, lean figure swaying slightly with the rocking of the boat, and cast his line out into the black swell just seaward of the waves. He looked at her, smiling like a happy schoolboy, and asked her if she was having a good time. She nodded, a lump forming in her throat preventing her from speaking. Happiness welled up inside her, blotting out everything else.

A cry from Huntley signaled that he had a bite. He pulled in his line—a primitive affair without a rod borrowed from one of the villagers—and on the end was a baby octopus. Claudia laughed when she saw it, and commented on what a fine fisherman he was. At that, he chased her, jumping over the crossbars of the boat, coming to wave the disgusting creature in her face. But then he tripped and fell into the water and they both laughed themselves silly.

That night Claudia both laughed and wept in her sleep . . .

CHAPTER SEVEN

The seven Germans stood in a respectful group outside the largest and most ornate brick temple in Bali, listening to Huntley Fox's explanation of the commotion going on around them. From inside the temple came the insistent clanging of a metal *gamelan,* tempered by the rhythmic thump of wooden percussion. A throng of people milled around the entrance, mostly women in clean sarongs and waist binders of scarlet or azure or cinnamon. Their long black hair, which usually hung loosely down their backs, today was twirled high into elegant knots pinned with gardenia or hibiscus blossoms. All were carrying an offering, the most common being a six-foot tower of rice cakes, each cake stained a different color with vegetable dye, the tower topped with a crudely painted portrait of Dewi Sri, the goddess of rice and fertility. Excitement was mounting on all sides.

"Before taking you to see the beginnings of my cultural center," Huntley was saying, "I thought you would want to come here to watch the celebration of the Festival of Dewi Sri. I obtained permission this morning from the *pemankah* of this temple, so we will now go inside and join with the Balinese in their interesting mixture of religion and fun."

"If it's the harvest they're celebrating," said Frau Steiner, "of course it's a time of great joy. What would they do without their rice?"

"I imagine they think of fertility as fun too," added Claudia with a naughty twinkle. "Don't they, Huntley? After all, we do, don't we?"

"You'll see when you get inside," he replied, his twinkle matching hers in a rare exhibition of humor that Claudia thoroughly enjoyed.

The manager led his group in single file through the crowded entrance to the temple. Once he was inside the broad courtyard fringed with palm fronds, his hand was solemnly shaken by the *pemankah,* even more magnificent than his colleague in Bedulu in his robes and glittering helmet. Huntley passed a roll of paper money to the *pemankah,* the size of which brought a gold-toothed smile to the man's face. Immediately he summoned an assistant, who supplied the guests with royal blue sashes to tie around their waists; Huntley explained that this was obligatory apparel for visitors to the temple. The assistant then led them to a raised dais in a corner from which they could watch the proceedings.

As they arrived, the offerings were placed in rows around the temple walls. Many were huge arrangements of fruit and flowers, and the drab crumbling brick soon became invisible behind a riot of color and form. Cries and laughter mixed with the pounding music of the *gamelan*. A wooden altar at the back supported two giant incense burners whose smoke curled upward; behind them stood a larger-than-life-size picture of Dewi Sri, executed in garish colors in the style of a cheap movie poster. The reproduction was identical to all the other portraits of the goddess, with her dark red skin, tiny features, and fan-shaped headdress, a bright-eyed smile forever blessing her worshipers.

A priest, clad in a loincloth, fussed around the altar, preparing for the arrival of the important men of the town. Claudia recognized the mailman by his uniform jacket worn over a gay patterned shirt; another wore an Indonesian airline cap over a bright embroidered shirt; a government inspector's high-necked coat topped a long *kamben*. Each profession had sent its senior representative to come forward and squat in a place of honor at the foot of the altar, but in each case some kind of gaiety had been added to the man's usual office garb.

Knowing what was expected of him as chief hotelier, Huntley Fox took his place on the ground alongside the other celebrities, a brilliant flower in his lapel serving as his personal frippery. To the music of the *gamelan* and the chanting of the congregation, the priest went through a short ritual of reception for each man, who then got up from the dusty floor and returned to his place.

"I can see you've been through this before," Claudia whispered to Huntley as he came back to her side.

"Yes, I find it interesting," he replied. "By participating, we gain the confidence of the Balinese so much better than if we remained aloof. That's one of the things my uncle doesn't understand."

"Well, I'm on your side, if it's any consolation," said Claudia.

He smiled at her rather wanly. "I'm glad to know that. But I'm afraid it won't make much difference to the outcome."

At that moment a tumultuous cheer went up from the multitude who jammed the temple. A procession of young girls, each bare-shouldered and with hair decorated by a bunch of flowers, moved into the courtyard and moved slowly around, receiving accolades from the groups of men they passed.

"This is the procession of virgins," Huntley informed his group. "Every family is required to contribute a specimen, but as you can see, some families have to lower the age limit a good deal in order to be able to comply." It was true; some families were represented by mere toddlers. "Now," the manager went on, "our group here is regarded as a family by these people. Who will be our representative virgin? Hilda Steiner, you are the youngest. Will you take these flowers and join the procession?" He held out a bouquet to the sturdy German girl as Claudia laughingly translated Huntley's request.

"I'm afraid I don't qualify," replied Hilda without a trace of embarrassment, although her parents looked quickly away. "I'm sorry."

117

"In that case it can only be Claudia here," Huntley went on, affixing the flowers to the head of the girl beside him. "I'm quite sure she qualifies."

"But . . . but I don't want to parade myself around in front of all those people. And anyway . . ."

It was too late for her protests. The bystanders on all sides had seen Huntley pin the flowers to her head and gently nudge her forward. A crescendo of cheers rose from all around her, and she had no alternative but to move into the procession and file around the courtyard, acclaimed wildly by all and sundry.

The moment the procession broke up, she dove back into the anonymity of the group, tearing off her floral adornment. "You . . . you beast to make me do that," she hissed at Huntley.

"Why? Surely you weren't guilty of impersonation, were you?" he inquired coolly.

"That's got nothing to do with you or with any of this," she growled.

"But it does, Claudia. You just finished telling me that you approved of the hotel's participating in the local customs. I did my bit by going out there with the other officials; you shouldn't complain about being our representative virgin. Unless of course . . ."

"Shut up!" she interrupted him. "Everybody's leaving. For goodness' sake, let's get out of here. I feel like an absolute fool."

The manager's party joined the shuffling crowd headed toward the entrance to the temple. As they passed the *pemankah*, they returned their sashes to him. The handsome young curator fixed Claudia with his dark, soulful eyes as he took hers, a question in them that made Claudia curse Huntley Fox once more under her breath.

Fortunately no further allusion was made to Claudia's part in the virginal procession, perhaps because the Germans were all too embarrassed by Hilda's blatant admission that she, at least, could not truthfully join the demonstration.

Huntley Fox now conducted them all to see his pet project on the outskirts of Denpasar, the Balinese Cultural Center. He envisaged a nicely landscaped area, like a park, which could house exhibitions by local artists, an open-air auditorium for theatrical performances, a woodcarving school, and examples of other local handicrafts. He felt that with the influx of tourism, the native people were becoming too materialistic to maintain their high cultural standards; as a hotel keeper largely responsible for the tourists, he considered it his duty to do what he could to preserve all that was best in the multifaceted Balinese culture. He carefully explained all this to his guests.

Then why does he import Negara from Jakarta to be his chief dancer, instead of searching out local girls such as Penebel? thought Claudia. When it comes to matters of the heart, reason flies out of the window, even for so dispassionate a person as Huntley Fox.

As the party walked around the center, Huntley proudly showed off the one building that was complete, the art gallery, and the Germans inspected with interest a show of primitive paintings by a young artist from Ubud.

"The prices are low enough," remarked Herr Hauptmann. "In Europe such complicated work involving hours of painstaking effort would cost at least two-hundred fifty dollars instead of only fifty dollars, as it is here."

"The artist is very happy to receive fifty dollars," said Huntley. "That's a lot of money to him, and because the Center makes no profit, he keeps every penny of it."

"But you could very easily make a profit by charging more," argued Hauptmann.

"That's what my Uncle Wilbur says. He thinks of this place as a sort of offshoot of Bali Breezes; he wants me to charge an entrance fee and top prices for all the artwork and handicrafts we sell, putting our profits into Malibu Hotels Limited, but I absolutely refuse to do that. Can you imagine how it would antagonize the local donors, to say nothing of the artists themselves? It would ruin the whole spirit of the Center."

It took a while for the smoldering outrage to die out of Huntley's dark eyes after they left the gallery and wandered through the pleasantly landscaped section surrounding a small lake. Here a little gravel path led up to a humped wooden bridge overhung with trees; it was a romantic spot and one that struck Frau Steiner as a suitable background for some group photographs. This prompted Hilda Steiner to insist on taking a shot of Huntley and Claudia by themselves. Claudia was hesitant, but Huntley whispered that they should satisfy their guests' whims, and led her onto the little bridge to lean over the rail side by side, grinning stupidly at the camera.

"*Nein, nein! Sie müssen liebkosen,*" commanded Hilda, squinting through the viewfinder.

"*Nicht so,*" replied Claudia with a smile. "*Wir sind nur Arbeiter.*"

"What did she say?" Huntley asked.

"Nothing. She wants us to snuggle up together, the silly girl."

"I'm afraid we have to follow our guests' every wish," said Huntley, squeezing Claudia to his side with a strong arm around her shoulders. "I hope you don't find it too distasteful."

"It's what happens to the print that I'm afraid of,"

replied Claudia, turning her face to look up at his as he gazed earnestly down at her, that being the moment that Hilda chose to open the shutter.

"*Sehr schön!*" said Hilda, turning on the film.

"That I understood," Huntley stated in a low voice, apparently in no hurry to release Claudia from his grip. "But I can only imagine that she means that you are very beautiful."

Wriggling away from him, the thought flashed through Claudia's mind that Huntley had acquiesced remarkably quickly to Hilda's request. He was normally such a reserved personality in public. Could it possibly be that it was a put-up job, that Hilda had been asked beforehand to take a compromising photo of the two of them? And that he would obtain the print from her later or arrange that some key members of the hotel staff would see it? Damn Negara's wretched theory about Huntley's duplicity! It was spoiling all Claudia's fun by making her imagination run riot.

"Tonight," announced Huntley to the assembled Germans, when they had arrived back at the hotel and gathered in the lobby, "tonight we are putting on a special barbecue dinner at the poolside, and afterward there will be music for dancing provided by the band that normally plays in the supper club. We are bringing the nightclub out of doors, for I am assured it will be a fine evening, and we would like to make it as memorable as we can for the Blums and the Hauptmanns, who will be leaving us tomorrow."

"That sounds excellent," said Frau Blum, with Claudia dutifully translating for Huntley's benefit. "As it is to be in our honor, the gentlemen in our party will wear tuxedos and the ladies ballgowns."

"That isn't really necessary . . ." the manager began.

"Maybe not, Mr. Fox," said Frau Blum with finality.

"But it's what we will do, just the same. We all have evening clothes with us for the formal occasions in Jakarta last week, and it would be a way of expressing our appreciation to you—and to Claudia—for a most enjoyable holiday."

The other Germans murmured their assent, as they always did after Frau Blum had spoken for them, and then moved off toward the elevators and their rooms.

"It's been a while since I wore my tux," Huntley said to Claudia. "I'd better get it pressed. And you'll wear a long skirt, okay?"

"Right," answered Claudia, although she didn't possess one. She didn't want to prolong the conversation; the lobby of the hotel was just too public a place to be seen chatting amiably with a manager who might be cruelly using her. She hurried off after the Germans.

Negara was lying stretched out on her bed in a filmy negligee, her bandaged foot resting on a pillow.

"Hi there, little miss," she greeted Claudia. "How has your lord and master been entertaining you today?"

"He hasn't been entertaining me. We've both been entertaining the German group. They're leaving tomorrow."

"Oh, they are? Doesn't that mean your job comes to an end too? Or are you being kept on for other purposes . . ." she suggested meaningfully.

"I'm sure you're all wrong about this business, Negara," said Claudia, settling herself on the edge of her bed. "But if by any chance someone on the staff mentions anything to you about it, would you tell me about it?"

"Of course I would, darling. And I'd put the person who told me straight about why the big show was being put on too, you can be sure of that. I don't want anybody getting ideas that he's interested in you, when they all already know that it's me he's after."

"Why not? I thought you didn't care about Huntley. I thought it was all you and Wilbur, and now that he's arrived here . . ."

"It is of course," said Negara quickly, pulling herself up to a sitting position. "But Wilbur's being a little slower than I would like. He hasn't actually proposed to me yet."

"But if he doesn't propose, Negara, if he goes back to the States without you, what will you do then?"

"We'll cross that bridge when we come to it," replied Negara, getting off the bed. "It's not really any business of yours anyway. Now, I'm going to take my bath. I want to look my best tonight . . . for both Wilbur and Huntley."

She went into the bathroom, leaving Claudia more confused than ever.

Her need for a long evening gown was resolved by a visit to the ground-floor boutique. A pretty off-the-shoulder dress in blue and cream velveteen fitted her perfectly, and went with the open-toed sandals she had bought there a couple of days ago. Claudia was well aware of the insecurity of her position at the hotel, whether Negara was right or not, and had no intention of squandering her earnings on clothes that would be useless the moment she was fired. Yet, she was determined that Huntley should notice her tonight! In letting her blond hair hang over her shoulders as it had the first night, she smiled inwardly at the thought that Huntley could not this time accuse her of grooming seductively for Anton. It would in fact be for his own benefit.

A large circular table had been prepared for the manager and his German guests. There was a refreshing cool breeze coming off the water, sending darkish clouds scudding across the moon.

Only the Hauptmanns were already at the table

when Claudia appeared. She sat down beside them and said she was sorry they would be leaving the next day.

"We have already spent too much money on this trip for the trade advantage my firm is likely to get out of it," said Herr Hauptmann.

"And we really prefer to take our vacation in more familiar surroundings," added his wife. "It has been most helpful having you here speaking German, Claudia, but I hate missing so much that is said by other people. One feels so out of place somehow. I will be glad to be home again among my own people."

The Blums and the Steiners arrived at about the time that the other tables began to fill up. The last to arrive was Huntley Fox, his mien as professorial in his tuxedo as when he wore his black alpaca jacket.

Huntley insisted on starting the evening by treating the whole party to champagne. He proposed a short toast to the three industrialists and their families, and Claudia was called upon to translate. Frau Blum replied with another toast, which Claudia summarized in English for Huntley. Then everyone linked arms in the European fashion and drank each others' health.

With their elbows locked and their glasses to their lips, Huntley's eyes met Claudia's and sent an unexpected shock wave down her spine. "You deserve a lot of the credit for the success of their visit," he said quietly. "Thank you, Claudia."

She lowered her soft brown lashes in shy acknowledgment of his thanks. Keeping their elbows linked, he followed up with, "And may I congratulate you on looking very beautiful tonight."

A hearty slap on his back made him spill some of his champagne. "Well said, my boy! Couldn't have put it better myself." Wilbur Fox stood behind his nephew, a tumbler of bourbon in his hand, a fat cigar between his teeth. Behind Wilbur, watching Huntley's discomfiture with amusement, were Anton and Negara. Negara was looking gorgeous in a black formfitting sheath.

The manager quickly disengaged his arm from Claudia's; then, seeing Negara, he rose to his feet. Wilbur pulled back Huntley's now vacant chair, ushered Negara into it, and pulled up another for himself. Anton took the only other empty chair, leaving Huntley with nowhere to sit. He glanced from one person to another around the table with a disconsolate expression and sauntered off, flicking the stray lock of hair back off his forehead.

"I'd like to introduce myself to the assembled company," Wilbur said to Claudia. "I guess you speak their lingo, so you do it for me, huh?"

Claudia cleared her throat and explained to the Germans that this was Mr. Wilbur Fox, the owner of the Malibu Hotel chain. She introduced each of the guests by name. Wilbur acknowledged them with a "Pleased to meetcha," and, with a flourish, presented Negara to them all. "An' this is a dear friend o' mine, the best dancer in the whole of the island of Bali, Miss Negara." The Germans inclined their heads stiffly and there was a pause until Anton said, *"Und ich bin Anton Reinholtz, der Hotelsportdirektor."*

Anton's knowledge of the German language broke the ice that had formed over the party since Wilbur's forceful entrance and Huntley's withdrawal. Soon the Blums and the Hauptmanns were loudly discussing with him the merits of various parts of Germany while Wilbur discussed the international hotel business with Herr Steiner. Negara sat between the two and Wilbur leaned across her, one hand resting casually on the shoulder nearest him, puffing cigar smoke in her face as he stated his categorical opinions. But the dancer didn't seem in the least disturbed by this arrangement; indeed she smiled benignly and even ventured an opinion of her own from time to time.

As soon as he could politely extricate himself from the two German couples, Anton turned urgently to Claudia at his side. "Claudia, *Liebchen!* So many days I do not see you! But now, now these people leave tomorrow, no? You will be free again for me."

"They're not all leaving, Anton. Frau Steiner and her daughter Hilda are staying on, and I'm going to have to entertain them. Unless you'd like to take Hilda over."

"That Hilda," said Anton out of the corner of his mouth, glancing across to where the girl sat looking voluptuously attractive in a blouson top and long striped skirt. "She is nice. I like her very much, but you, you spoil me for all the others. So tomorrow we swim together, no?"

"I'm sorry, Anton, I'll be busy," said Claudia abruptly, turning her back on him because she had overheard Frau Steiner trying to get her husband to explain something in German. "Excuse me, Frau Steiner, but Miss Negara is the regular dancer with the hotel troupe. It's only because she has sprained her ankle that Mr. Fox has hired the girl Penebel to take her place for a week or two."

"Whassat about me?" Wilbur blinked unsteadily at Claudia.

"I said nothing about you, sir," replied Claudia in a pacifying tone.

Wilbur took a swig of bourbon and finished his glass. "Yes, you did so. I heard you say Herr Fox—distinctly. Thash me, ain't it?"

"Oh, I see. No, I meant Mr. Huntley Fox, the manager. He has hired a young dancer from a village called Bedulu to take Negara's place until her ankle's better. Her name's Penebel and she's very good."

"*What* did you say?" A sudden pallor showed through Negara's makeup. "I've heard about this Penebel. The natives like her, but she's completely untrained. What on earth made Huntley take her on at the hotel? How did he come to hear about her?"

"As a matter of fact, I told him about her, and he came with us to watch her at Bedulu last night."

"*You* told him?" Negara's teeth gritted as she glared at Claudia across Wilbur's now almost insensible form. "Why, you little . . . But I suppose you didn't think. Anyway, I'm going to have to find that fool Huntley and have him cancel the girl. We can't have her here."

Negara spotted Huntley leaning over a table of laughing guests, and slunk over to join him, slipped an arm through his, and led him to one of the thatched umbrellas at the edge of the pool. There, half-hidden from the crowd, she could be seen running her hand up his arm, straightening his tie, and touching his chin with her long red fingernail. Huntley was making no effort to escape from Negara's attention. Watching, Claudia felt horribly, inexplicably jealous.

Anton followed the direction of her intense observation and commented on it. "Why you are so interested in the little scene over there, Claudia? Surely it not surprise you. Negara, she likes to keep both the Foxes happy."

"Oh, that's just gossip," said Claudia. "Look, why don't you take Hilda and her parents over to the buffet to help themselves?"

"Yes, it is time for food. I will do it if you also come to take from the barbecue."

"All right," Claudia agreed, glad for the diversion. The long trestle was laden with all kinds of delicacies, some Indonesian and others international. Claudia slipped from under Anton's hovering presence to consult with the elder Steiners about their selection. This left Anton unavoidably with Hilda, and the two of them were waiting under the buffet-table awning for their steaks to be barbecued when Claudia and the Steiners made their way back to the table.

Wilbur Fox woke up as they sat down and blinked at Claudia stupidly. "Guess I must have dropped off there for a minute."

"Why don't you help yourself to some food, Mr. Fox," she suggested. "It's really very good."

"I think I'll have myself a little drink first," Wilbur replied. Then he turned to the Steiners to ask, "Does this little girl spend all her time telling you what you should do? She does it to everyone else."

"Oh, no," said Herr Steiner. "My wife and daughter tell me that she has been the most excellent guide these last few days. Helpful but not overbearing."

Wilbur Fox brought Claudia into focus and inspected her with a new appreciation. "I'm certainly glad to hear that. Maybe my nephew did right to hire her, then. It seemed kinda waste of funds when I heard about it, but as long as she has kept you folks happy . . ."

Anton and Hilda joined them. Anton made a beeline for the empty seat beside Claudia, but Hilda took the one on his other side; Claudia hoped that her perseverance would eventually pay off.

Wilbur Fox rose unsteadily to his feet and went to refill his glass. The Steiners were eating with less concentration than their daughter, but still with obvious relish. Silence had descended upon the table when Claudia felt the first huge tropical raindrop. It splashed onto her head, and was quickly followed by others.

Chaos ensued. Screams rent the air as the diners

fled for cover, scooping up plates, glasses, and cutlery as they went. At Claudia's table everybody had so nearly finished their meal that they abandoned what little remained. The Steiners rushed off to shelter under the barbecue awning, but Anton seized Claudia's arm and propelled her toward one of the thatched umbrellas, not far from the one where Negara had been trying—Claudia knew not how successfully—to influence Huntley in the matter of a replacement dancer. Hilda hesitated for a moment, wondering whether to go with Anton and Claudia or with her parents. To Claudia's chagrin, she chose her parents, leaving her alone with Anton, separated from the great majority of the guests congregated under the awning by a wall of water, but nevertheless in full view of them from the overhead lights that had been strung around the pool.

"Why did you make me come here?" Claudia asked petulantly, looking up at the rough thatch above them. "This thing's going to start leaking like a sieve in a minute."

"No, it will keep us dry if we stand here in the middle." Anton put an arm around her waist and tried to draw her to him, but she firmly put his arm away.

"Anton, the whole world can see us from under that awning over there. Please keep your hands to yourself."

"But, *Liebchen,* I want to talk with you about us, you and me. Will you not be my regular friend? Will you spend your not-working time with me?"

"No, Anton, I'm sorry but the answer is no. I'm quite happy to be friends with you, but that's all. Besides, I'll probably only be here another week or so, until the Steiners leave."

"But then we can start the dance classes, remember. I will speak with Wilbur Fox about my idea. He will tell the manager it must be done." Anton rubbed his hands together gleefully.

"Don't you dare do any such thing!" Claudia said angrily. "If I stay on at this hotel in any capacity, it can only be at the request of the manager. I wouldn't dream of letting you go behind his back to keep me here."

"But what does it matter, *Liebchen?* It would not even be necessary for you ever to see Huntley Fox—it is for me that you would be working."

"But you work for Huntley, don't you? And anyway, I like being on his personal staff. It's interesting and I enjoy it, so I hope he asks me to stay on. But I wouldn't consider any other arrangement."

Anton looked at her quizzically. "It is not the Mister Fox that you find interesting, is it? Because if it is, you must surely know that he only has the eyes for Negara. You waste your time if . . ."

The sentence was never finished, because suddenly the outdoor entertainment area was plunged into darkness. Only the distant lights in the windows of the hotel continued to burn through the sheets of rain that still pelted down. Screams and laughter vied with the incessant patter of drops on the concrete at their feet and the straw matting above. It was dark, and Claudia felt Anton's hand again groping for her. She wondered whether to run for the safety of the crowd under the awning . . .

"Anton!" A tall shadow materialized beside them, and Anton quickly withdrew his questing hand. "Anton, go to the hotel and fetch the electrician. Tell him I want these lights fixed immediately."

"But, Huntley,"—even in the darkness it was easy to tell who it was who had joined them—"my new pants they will so wet become. Cannot one of the waiters go?"

"No, the waiters are busy. I want you to go—at once!"

When the manager barked out an order, Anton obeyed without question.

Her eyes were beginning to become used to the darkness, and Huntley's form beside her gradually took on more substance.

"I saw Anton drag you here when the rain began," he said. "I hope he wasn't bothering you."

No more than Negara was bothering you under one of these umbrellas a few minutes ago, thought Claudia. Aloud she said, "Oh, no, not really. Being alone with any girl sets off a sort of chemical reaction in Anton. I'm sure I'm much safer with you, aren't I?"

"I'm not entirely immune to female charms, you know."

"As long as they don't interfere with your work as a hotel manager, isn't that right? With you your duties always come first, don't they? And at this moment you're still very much in charge here, even in the dark under an umbrella with a girl and the rain pouring down outside."

"Absolutely, Claudia," he replied emphatically, but she could detect a hint of amusement in his voice.

"I'll bet you've even got your manager's glasses on," she teased him.

"You're quite right. I have."

A small devil took charge of Claudia. She reached up toward the shadow of Huntley's head, and whisked the plain-glass spectacles from his nose, hiding them behind her back. "There! Now you're not a manager anymore."

"Hey! Give me those back," he cried.

"No, you'll have to come and get them. I've got them behind my back."

She felt him touch her shoulder; a shiver of excitement ran through her. Would he respond to her teasing?

"Claudia, please!" he begged. "The lights might go on at any minute and then everybody would know my secret about the glasses."

"Oh, no, it'll take the electrician hours to fix them in this downpour. I doubt if he'll even be bothered to come out in it."

"He'll come out in any weather, I promise you. He's a very conscientious worker. Give me those glasses back!"

"You can have them if you come and get them," laughed Claudia. "I told you they're behind my back."

His arms enfolded her, and she reached further backward with the glasses to bring him closer. His body pressed firmly against hers now; she could feel his breath on her cheek. His unruly lock of hair brushed across her forehead. She instinctively reached up with her face, as his hands ceased trying to find the glasses and closed around her back, holding her resolutely.

She slipped her hands up, and crossed them behind his neck. "Isn't this more fun than being a manager?" she panted, her heart racing now.

"Infinitely." His voice came to her out of the dark, soft and tender, only an inch from her face. Then his mouth found hers, and strong forceful lips moved gently over hers, fitting them together until they were locked in the mounting passion of an embrace that carried Claudia into another world. Still Huntley held her, unwilling or unable to let her go, urgently exploring . . .

The light immediately outside their umbrella went on. The rest of the area was still in darkness, and from the crowded barbecue awning, a great gasp came to them, followed by gales of laughter and ribald comments.

Huntley and Claudia broke apart as if stung. He seized his glasses and replaced them on his nose, sweeping back his forelock.

"Oh, my God!" he said. "I've really done it now. I'll never live this one down."

"I think everybody will be pleased to find their hotel manager is human after all," replied Claudia. "I certainly am for one. That was quite delicious, thank you very much."

"All right," he said, an artificial smile creasing his face. "We'll just make a joke out of it; that's the best way." He waved jovially at the crowd and raised Claudia's hand as if she was the winner of some tournament, but not many people saw him, because all the other lights went on at the same instant, distracting people's attention.

The rain stopped as suddenly as it had begun. Houseboys in bare feet scurried around, wiping the water off the tables and chairs, and mopping the dance floor. The guests ventured out of their hiding places and resumed eating and drinking under the stars.

Huntley left Claudia immediately and without a word headed for the hotel; Claudia smiled to herself, partly from the pleasure that remained from his kiss, and partly at the thought of his not being able to face the remarks and jokes that would be made at his expense if he stayed around. She herself felt nothing to be embarrassed about, but in point of fact, it seemed that only strangers had actually witnessed the embrace. None of the Germans gave any sign of having seen it when they had all resumed their seats at the table. Fortunately, Anton hadn't caught them either—he certainly would have commented if he had.

But Negara had seen, and she drew Claudia aside as soon as they had sat down. "Now do you believe me?" she opened the conversation earnestly. "That kiss he gave you was rigged. He knew the lights were about to come on again. You know that, don't you?"

"Don't be silly," said Claudia. "Frankly I made it easy for him. I held his glasses behind my back."

"All the same," said Negara with emphasis, "I'm absolutely convinced he wouldn't have gone along with your little game except for one reason. I told you, I'm the only girl he has the slightest interest in."

Although Claudia didn't really believe Negara, she felt curiously deflated by the thought that Huntley might not have kissed her for genuine pleasure. There seemed only one way to find out once and for all if Negara was right and that was to flirt with Anton, and see how Huntley reacted.

When the band started up, Claudia accepted with alacrity Anton's invitation to dance, and stayed with him most of the evening. Huntley Fox was present nearly all the time, but he took no notice of Claudia, leaving her baffled as to the reason.

CHAPTER EIGHT

The next morning Claudia received a message from Eleanor Davis to attend a farewell coffee party for the departing Germans. Herr Blum and Herr Hauptmann made their usual hand-kissing gestures, and their wives solemnly shook hands with her. Then they were gone, leaving Claudia standing rather awkwardly in front of Huntley's desk.

"This afternoon I'd like to take you on that trip in my copter up to Mount Agung."

Claudia remained silent, her mind in a turmoil. If she was convinced that Huntley was just using her as a decoy to allay the hotel staff's suspicions about him and Negara, this was the moment for her to hand in her resignation. But if this wasn't true at all, then all the more reason for her to stay and accept this exciting invitation. She decided to test him by mentioning Anton.

"Well, don't you want to go?" He looked up at her impatiently.

"Would it be just you and me?"

"I thought so, yes. I told you, I wanted your opinion on whether it would be a suitable jaunt for women guests as well as men. That's why we'd be going."

"I see," said Claudia slowly. "Because I was wondering whether we could take Anton Reinholtz along too. You're planning the trip as guest entertainment, and he is entertainment director after all."

Huntley's jaw jutted forward and a crease formed on his brow. "Is it necessary for you to be accompanied by Anton everywhere you go except on assignments from me?"

"No, of course not, but I . . ."

"I noticed you spent practically the whole evening dancing with him last night. I would much prefer that you distributed your charms more evenly. I don't want any rumors about you and Anton any more than I want rumors about you and me."

Claudia giggled in relief. These were not the words of someone who was using her. "There wouldn't be much chance for rumors about me and Anton after what everyone saw when the lights went up last night."

Huntley coughed, and then looked at her over his glasses, the corner of his mouth curling in a half-smile. "Yes, that was an unfortunate coincidence, but I don't think too many people saw, and those that did would have realized it was just a playful little game."

"I'm glad about that. I wouldn't want anyone to think otherwise. And, yes, I'd be delighted to go up to the volcano with you this afternoon."

"Good. Meet me down at the helicopter pad just off the beach at two o'clock. But be inconspicuous."

Claudia waited as directed, and right on time Huntley appeared and they climbed in together. A few moments later the helicopter rose effortlessly from its pad, the giant blades slicing the air above them. The pool, the beach, the golf course, the whole hotel complex rapidly shrank in size until it was no more than a small cultivated area carved out of the forest.

Away to the west, the town of Denpasar was a brown smudge, and beyond it Claudia could make out the golden swath that was Kuta Beach and the dark blue ocean lost in haze on the horizon. Then they headed northeast over the emerald rice paddies, their steep terraces foreshortened from the air. Closely packed *kampongs* of thatched-roofed houses, each hamlet clustered around a brick temple, were dotted across the hillside or wedged into the valleys. The lush beauty of the country was revealed even more breathtakingly from above than at ground level.

"When I'm flying over Bali," said Huntley, "I feel like the god Wismu riding on the back of the mythical bird Garuda."

"I've seen carvings of that scene. You must know even more about the Balinese people and their culture than I told the Germans you did."

"I find it very interesting. One of the things the Muslim Indonesians haven't been able to wipe out is the rigid caste system. The highest caste are addressed as *tjokorda,* which means 'feet.' Lower people must kneel and speak to 'your honor's feet' without looking at their faces. It's a strictly enforced *adat.*"

"What's an *adat?*"

"A custom so strong that it's an unwritten law. There's another one that you wouldn't like at all." Huntley took his eyes off the controls for a moment to throw Claudia a wry smile. "It says that a woman is of secondary importance to a man. Men aren't allowed to ill-treat their wives, but the wives must obey their husbands in all matters."

"I don't think I'd mind that. If I ever got married, it would have to be to someone I respected so much that I would want to obey him."

"Even to not making a fuss if he took a second wife?"

"Are the Balinese allowed more than one wife?"

"Absolutely. Not only by their religion but by Indonesian law also. It's one of the most attractive features of life on this island."

"Huntley!" cried Claudia aghast. "You mean you'd like to have two wives?"

"Well, it saves having to make a choice if there are two girls one is fond of."

"And are there two girls you're fond of?"

"No, I think there's only one."

"What's she like?" asked Claudia, as if she didn't know.

"Slim, graceful, beautiful, a dancer. The only trouble is that she doesn't always want to follow the *adat,* the one that says she must obey me."

That's for sure, thought Claudia, recalling the rude, vicious way Negara had spoken to him the day she sprained her ankle. "Talking of dancers," said Claudia innocently, "is Penebel dancing the *ramayana* ballet tonight at the hotel?"

"Oh, yes. She came down this morning and is rehearsing with our group right now."

Claudia breathed a sigh of relief at his reassuring reply, as Huntley suddenly swung the ungainly machine he was flying to the right. Down below lay the holy temple of Besakih, flattened against the slope of the mountain, and straight ahead loomed the conical peak of Mount Agung itself, nearly ten thousand feet above sea level, its upper half devoid of vegetation, black with solidified lava.

Huntley lowered the helicopter with infinite care onto a small, level piece of ground not far from the edge of the crater. He switched off the engine and opened the door on his side of the cabin. A blast of freezing air blew in; Claudia shuddered and pulled on the heavy sweater she had brought with her. Huntley got out, came around to her side, and helped her down. The crust of lava crumbled slightly under her feet, causing her to cry out, fearful that this insubstantial ground might give way altogether and plunge her into some murky place below.

"Hold up there!" called Huntley, gripping her hand tightly. "It's all right, it's only the surface that breaks when you tread on it. It's quite firm underneath."

He led her toward the edge of the crater. Climbing over the uneven rim, they peered inside. Claudia felt like an astronaut setting foot on some strange planet. The black malevolent pool of lava stretched several hundred feet across, fissured and cracked like a dried-up lake of stinking mud. Wisps of steam broke through and bubbled as they watched.

"Ugh! It's like a witch's caldron," said Claudia. "Are you sure it isn't about to erupt again?"

"Quite sure. I wouldn't risk bringing guests up here if there were any chance of that, believe me. But tell me, do you think the ladies would be interested in seeing it?"

"Interested, yes. But it would scare the daylights out of some of them. You're going to have to provide a manly hand for each one of them to give them confidence—like this." She held up the hand that was clasped in his and, laughing, looked into his steady dark-brown eyes.

He looked down at her, smiling under his bushy brows, and, releasing her hand, slipped his own around her shoulders, drawing her firmly to his side. "Maybe this would give them even more reassurance."

"You're going to be busy, if you give this kind of treatment to all the female guests you bring up here."

He gave her shoulder a final squeeze and then led her back away from the crater. "Come on, I'd better get you down to the seaside before you catch your death of cold."

They climbed back into the cockpit and pulled the Plexiglas shield over them. It was much warmer inside.

But instead of starting the motor immediately, he turned to gaze thoughtfully at Claudia. "Are you at all frightened, flying with me in this machine?"

"Oh, no, not a bit! It's just the places you take me to that are scary. Why?"

"Well, what are you going to do with yourself now that nearly all the Germans have left?"

"That's up to you. I gather you want me to stay on and look after the Steiners, though I'm trying to arrange for Anton to keep Hilda occupied instead of me. She likes him quite a bit."

"And you're promoting the relationship? That's funny, I thought you liked Anton quite a bit yourself."

"Well, he's okay, but not my type nearly as much as he's hers."

"What is your type, then, Claudia?"

"That I'll tell you when he comes along. I have no very fixed ideas on the subject. I'm much more interested in what people are like underneath than what they seem to be on the outside. First impressions can be very misleading."

Huntley didn't seem to be listening. "Anton's good-looking, athletic, amusing, attentive," he said. "I find it hard to believe that you don't reciprocate his obvious interest in you." His eyes narrowed as he added, "Are you sure you're not just promoting the relationship between him and Hilda Steiner in order to distract the attention of the gossipmongers on the hotel staff, so that they are unaware of your relationship with him? You're safe to do so, because she's leaving soon."

Claudia stared at Huntley in amazement, then burst out laughing. "That's really funny—your suggesting that might be my motive." Now she was sure it couldn't be the motive for his attentions and kisses either. He would never have mentioned it if it were.

"Funny? Why? I don't understand." His brow creased.

"I'm sorry, Huntley, I can't tell you. But I promise it isn't true about me. For one thing, I don't have enough guile for that sort of deception."

"Good. I don't like scheming females."

Oh, Huntley! Claudia thought. If only he could know that the object of his devotion was the most scheming female she had ever come across. Aloud she asked, "Why did you ask me just now if I was frightened flying with you?"

"Oh, yes." He relaxed and ran his hand along the back of her seat. "Well, I was wondering if you'd like to take another trip with me in this aircraft—a longer one."

Lights shone in her amber eyes. "Sure, I'd love to. Where would we go to, and when?"

"The island of Borneo. The nearest part of it is about two hundred miles due north of here, but we'd be going to a place on the Skrang River, about a hundred miles farther on. It would take about five hours each way in the copter."

"Sounds fascinating. Would this be just a pleasure trip?"

"Of course not! It would be part of your job to accompany me, just as today's run up here has been. You see, my Uncle Wilbur is always on the lookout for new locations to build hotels, and somebody has told him about the Ibans—they're the native race who live on the Skrang River—and how interesting they are to the more adventurous tourists."

"So he's thinking of putting up a Malibu International Hotel there, is that it?"

"Exactly. At the moment, the nearest place to stay is a town called Kuching, nearly six hours away by rough road and canoe. Wilbur thinks that if we put a hotel right on the spot, we'd capture the whole market of people coming to see how the Ibans live."

"And what's so remarkable about that?" asked Claudia.

"Well, they live in huge wooden buildings called longhouses, a kind of communal life for about twenty families, up to a hundred people altogether. These longhouses are strung out all along the river, one every mile or so, and the Ibans farm the surrounding bush country, mostly with rice and pepper trees."

"That sounds as though it would be worth a visit, but does it have enough attraction to keep a hotel full all year round?"

"Wilbur wants me to see for myself and bring him back a report. As a hotel man, I might be biased; that's why I thought I'd take you with me—to get the point of view of a woman tourist."

"It sounds like tremendous fun, but I'm sure we'll decide that some primitive natives living in wooden huts wouldn't be nearly interesting enough to make it worthwhile building a hotel miles from anywhere else. It can't be like Bali, with all its other attractions."

"You may well be right," Huntley nodded, as he put his hand to the ignition switch. "But there is one other thing about the Ibans that has a certain weird appeal."

"What's that?"

"They are headhunters. That means that each young man has to cut off the head of an enemy before he is accepted into the tribe. The longhouses are said to have human heads hanging from the ceilings all through them."

"What?" Claudia shrank back in horror.

"I believe they've given up the practice now, so the skulls are all pretty old and unrecognizable, but it does give the place a sort of macabre fascination."

"Well, count me in, headhunters or not. When do we go?"

"Would tomorrow be all right?" But he didn't wait to hear her acceptance, because he turned the key and the powerful engine leaped into noisy life. A few moments later, in a cloud of black lava dust from the churning propeller, they swung off the mountaintop. Within half an hour they had landed at the Bali Breezes Hotel.

Wilbur Fox appeared to have been lying in wait for them; he waddled up and accosted them almost as soon as they had their feet on the ground.

"Ah, there you are, my boy. Taking the young lady

for a spin, eh? I'm surprised you trust your life with him in that contraption, Claudia."

"He's as good a pilot as he is a manager," said Claudia crisply. "So I felt perfectly safe."

Wilbur shook his head as if to get it working better. "Can't think of an answer to that right now. Be better when I've had a drink." He adjusted his dark glasses.

"Did you want to see me about something?" Huntley asked Wilbur. "Because if not . . ."

"Yes, two things, as a matter of fact," replied his uncle, wiping the sweat from under the rim of his baseball cap. "First, I was watching that girl you brought down from the mountains rehearse this afternoon. Negara took me along; she thinks the girl's terrible and wants me to get you to fire her. But I couldn't agree. To tell you the truth, I thought she was better than Negara herself. But of course I wasn't going to tell her that."

"Very interesting," said Huntley flatly. "And the second thing?"

"Oh, yes, I think I'll be moving on to Australia in a day or two, so I'll need your report on that Borneo situation as soon as possible."

"You'll have it in forty-eight hours, Uncle. I'm going over there tomorrow, and will be back the following afternoon. You'll have the benefit of Claudia's opinion too, as I intend to take her along."

"Well, all right," said Wilbur grudgingly. "I suppose that's not a bad idea, now that nearly all the German party have left. After that, I imagine you'll be letting her go. Never pay for useless staff."

"Uncle, I think you should know that Miss Bauer has worked extremely hard the last few days—much harder, I may say, than Anton Reinholtz. If there's anyone who should be let go . . ."

"I might be taking that young lad off your hands one of these days soon. He was talking to me about it. Seems he's kind of anxious to get back to Europe, and I think I might be able to oblige."

Huntley shot a look at Claudia.

"Oh, Mr. Fox, I think that's a marvelous idea," said Claudia. "Anton is such a good skier; he really ought to be employed in one of your Swiss resort hotels. The sooner you get him there, the better." She gave Huntley a brief challenging glance, and was relieved to see that he was having trouble suppressing a smile.

"Well, I don't know what it's got to do with you, young lady," said Wilbur, slightly taken aback. "Anyways, I'll be leaving it to the manager here to dispose of you when you've outgrown your usefulness."

"You can be sure I'll do that," said Huntley.

"I'm sure he will," added Claudia, as sweetly as she could.

On the way up to her room in the elevator, Claudia mulled over the manager's new invitation. Or was it an invitation? Wasn't it an assignment, just like all the other assignments he had given her? A sudden thought struck her. Did Wilbur leaving so soon mean that he was taking Negara with him as she was desperately hoping? With Negara out of the way, Huntley's infatuation would soon pass, and that special place in his heart would again become available.

Did Claudia want that place in his heart for herself? she wondered. Could she cope with a man who behaved like a haughty monarch one minute and like a puckish clown the next? It was like being in love with two people at the same time.

To Claudia's surprise, she found Negara in their room, sprawled across the single easy chair, her bandaged leg up on the bed, her hair hanging limply, and her face sporting no makeup. Her expression was a mixture of anger and resolve. She was working on her fingernails with a grim concentration.

"Hello, Negara." Claudia threw herself down and stretched out on her own bed. "I've just been on the most fantastic trip. Huntley took me up to the top of Mount Agung in his whirlybird."

"I must get him to take me some time. It would be my first step to making him like me as well as worship me. That's the next item on my agenda."

"I didn't think you cared whether he liked you or not. You seemed to . . ." A sudden thought hit Claudia. She sat up. "You're not trying to work on him some more to get him to fire Penebel, are you? Because if you are, I'm warning you, I'm going to put up some tough opposition."

"Darling, don't get so excited! No, I don't care if he wants to employ the little novice from the country for a few days until this stupid leg gets better. No, I just want him to start thinking of me as more than a mere gorgeous hunk of flesh. He's got to start looking to me for companionship, maybe even the lifelong variety."

Claudia's jaw dropped open, but Negara didn't notice; she was still busy with her nails. "But I thought you were all set with Uncle Wilbur, and didn't give a toot about Huntley."

"That was until about an hour ago, darling. The old lecher has reneged on me. Taken all the favors and not come up with the reward. He's not taking me back to the States with him after all."

"So you're going to make a play for Huntley now, is that it?" asked Claudia, careful to modulate her voice so that she sounded almost bored.

"Right. He does have the advantage of being better-looking. See—I always look on the bright side."

Claudia remained silent, afraid that anything she said might give away the fact that she wasn't entirely disinterested in this new turn of events.

Negara went on. "By the way, as Huntley and I get thicker, he'll be more anxious than ever to hide it from the staff, so you can expect him to want to be seen around with you even more. I'm just telling you so that you can be prepared for it and not think that it means anything."

"Of course not," said Claudia.

"Good," said Negara sweetly. Negara looked up at Claudia for the first time. "We really understand each other, don't we, darling?"

"I think so," said Claudia, feeling a wave of nausea come over her. She couldn't stay in this room any longer listening to Negara's plans to win Huntley away from her. Away from her? Since when was the manager hers for anybody to win away? She tried to be rational and cool about the situation while she changed into her swimsuit and left Negara's stifling presence.

As a place of escape, where she could sort through her feelings, Claudia chose a secluded patch of grass behind a flowering shrub in the hotel garden. There she lay prone on her towel, resting her head on her arms, pretending to be asleep, wanting to be left in peace.

But Claudia was far from asleep and far from at peace. A turmoil of thoughts and emotions struggled for supremacy in her worried mind. Yet one clear, inescapable fact shone through like a beacon. She was in love with Huntley Fox. Both the Huntley Foxes. The meticulous stickler and the free spirit.

Negara still blithely assumed that Claudia's presence in the hotel depended entirely on her value to Huntley as a means of diversion of public opinion away from his real attachment; Claudia didn't care whether Negara was right or not. She loved Huntley anyway.

The trip to Borneo, planned for tomorrow, could easily be part of her role as rumor-bait. Surely it wasn't really necessary for him to take her along; one of the junior executives could give just as valuable advice. Yet it was an excursion that would be bound to attract a good deal of attention and talk.

So much so, in fact, that Huntley might—if this was indeed his plan—be defeating his own ends. Whether his act was intentional or not, it might well induce a round of false and idle gossip that would be just as harmful as the truth about Negara. It was plainly apparent that Huntley Fox felt very strongly that he couldn't maintain strict discipline over his employees if there were snickers behind his back about his affairs of the heart. He had to appear to be above all that sort of thing. Therefore it must appear that neither Claudia nor Negara was his particular favorite.

How, then, to protect him from the embarrassment he so dreaded? Not only must he and the rest of the world never have an inkling of the way she felt about him but they must think that her heart belonged to another. The obvious thing to do was to cease denying her interest in Anton. At the next opportunity she would tell Huntley that she had at last succumbed to Anton's good looks, virility, and persuasive manner; and she would allow herself to be seen around with him enough to substantiate the story in everyone's eyes. She now hoped Anton's transfer would be delayed.

It would be torture, sheer hell, to live this double lie, pretending that Huntley meant nothing to her, but she would do it until Negara forced an open admission from Huntley that wedding plans were on the way. Then she, Claudia, would quietly retire from the whole scene to nurse her broken heart.

Her plan thus formulated, she began to think about the visit to Borneo and the headhunters, scheduled for tomorrow. Curiously, it made her feel better. The idea of traveling alone with Huntley to a distant island for exploration and adventure banished temporarily the gloom of earlier thoughts. She determined to enjoy his company to the full, even if it was to be for the last time.

CHAPTER NINE

The coastline of Borneo loomed gradually closer. A lazy river emptied a crescent of brown silt into the turquoise shallows of the South China Sea; in the distance blue mountains were fringed with cloud. There was no sign of human habitation.

Claudia's sense of adventure, born in the hotel garden yesterday afternoon, had heightened since their takeoff, and she had been glowing with anticipation since Huntley had sent her a message to be prepared for an overnight trip.

Even Negara's appearance in the hotel lobby had scarcely deflated Claudia's buoyant spirit. Huntley hadn't specifically told her to meet him at the helicopter pad, so she had lain in wait for him in the lobby, ready to fulfill her role as hoax lover, arranging to be seen going off with him. In due course he had stepped from the elevator, carrying a small bag.

Negara had no intention of letting him depart for

a couple of days without bidding him a fond farewell. "I'll be counting the hours till you come back, my sweetness," she purred into Huntley's ear, linking her arm through his. He stiffened slightly, apparently embarrassed, thought Claudia. To ease the situation for him and to confuse any curious onlookers, Claudia slipped her arm through his other one, a gesture that brought a smile of appreciation from him. Thus linked, the three of them marched conspicuously through the crowded lobby.

As soon as they had passed through the lobby and were outside and away from the crowds of people, Claudia let go of Huntley's arm, leaving Negara in full possession. They walked along the ramp that led to the helicopter pad, Claudia tactfully a few paces behind. Reaching the machine, she climbed quickly into the passenger seat, seeing out of the corner of her eye the tender kiss that Negara planted on Huntley's lips. She was relieved to notice that Huntley seemed unwilling to prolong the affectionate farewell, even in the comparative privacy of the landing ground. He clambered up beside Claudia and immediately shut the doors and covering shield.

A few moments later Negara had fled from the downdraft of the rotor blades and they had lifted off into the clear blueness above them. Now, about three hours later, they were crossing the coast of Borneo.

"I'm looking forward to seeing what kind of people the Iban are," Huntley said. "They have a reputation for violence quite unlike the Balinese. Yet the Balinese can be murderers too in a more subtle way. I'll give you an example. You know, when a village puts on a cockfight girls from the neighborhood come and set up lemonade stalls for the men. Not long ago there was a very pretty girl who did this in a village called Duda. She naturally attracted most of the business away from the other girls, including the daughter of one of the market ladies. The pretty girl bought her lunch from this lady and a short time later collapsed to the ground and died. Everybody knew that she had been poisoned, but nobody raised a finger to help her, and even the doctor certified that she had died of cholera."

"What an awful story!" cried Claudia. "Why didn't someone speak up if they suspected poisoning?"

"Because the whole village bought food from that market lady, and they were afraid that if they did the same fate might befall them."

"And all because the woman was jealous of the girl's looks?"

"That's right," said Huntley, smiling at her. "Silly, isn't it? Everybody knows that no man in his right mind is going to be seriously influenced by a woman's appearance. A passing attraction, perhaps, but no more. It's the invisible qualities that count."

"Like honesty?" asked Claudia. "And a genuine involvement in a man's hopes and dreams?"

"Exactly. Those are the things I hope to find in a girl before I ask her to marry me. I think that maybe I've already found them. And the girl is gorgeous too. Aren't I lucky?"

"I . . . I hope you're right," muttered Claudia, biting her lip so that the pain might deaden her feeling of hopeless frustration. To change the subject she added, "Are we going to fly over those mountains ahead of us?"

"That's right," he answered brightly. "The Skrang River is on the other side of that range. Actually the mountains form the border between Indonesia and Malaysia, so the longhouses are in another country."

"Oh, dear!" cried Claudia. "I forgot to bring my passport."

"That's all right," Huntley reassured her. "There are

no border guards in this wild part of the world. And we won't be going into Malaysia officially, so we don't need any documents. That's why we have to spend the night at the longhouse—we can't fly on into the town of Kuching to sleep at the hotel there, because we'd be nabbed at the airport without visas. Anyway it's a lot farther to go."

"So we're going to sleep with these headhunters?" Her voice betrayed her alarm.

"Well, I don't know who you're going to sleep with. . . ." Huntley gave her an amused smile.

Claudia felt herself blushing. "I didn't mean that. I was only scared they might slaughter us in our beds."

"Don't worry. The visitors from Kuching sleep at the longhouses and seem to get home safely. But of course they have guides with them."

"How are we going to talk to them without a guide?"

"Malaysia used to be a British colony, so some of them will speak English. That's one of the advantages of building a hotel here."

"I see. But I still don't think I'll get a wink of sleep all night if I'm alone with some lady headhunters."

"Do you think you'd be safer with me?" Huntley was grinning at her again.

"What is the fate worse than death? None that I know of." She smiled back at him, happy that he was softening and becoming human once more.

"In that case I'll ask that we share a room. But don't tell anyone when we get back to Bali."

"I won't," she promised. "Not a soul will know."

The helicopter skimmed over the ridge of mountains, and a great wooded plain spread out in front of them. Winding across the plain, partly hidden by the jungle that flourished on its banks, was the river, and as they descended from the ridge, a series of thatched wooden buildings came into view about a mile apart, built high on tall stilts above the water level, each as long as an American motel. The noise of their machine brought old women and children, brown and almost naked, out of each longhouse as they passed over it. The men and younger women working the rice paddies, both sexes stripped to the waist, also looked up as they passed overhead, but the Iban had seen aircraft before, and showed no more than a passing interest.

"The longhouse we want is just round that next bend in the river," said Huntley. "Let's hope there's a nice flat spot beside it where we can land."

Huntley held the helicopter poised for a moment over the longhouse he had chosen, and then let it down, aiming for a patch of dry ground. Children scattered, their hands over their ears, as the ungainly chopper came closer, and the leaves of the palms and other tall trees waved furiously in the downthrust. Finally it settled, not fifty yards from the primitive building.

A crude ladder led eight feet up from ground level to the entrance. There Huntley and Claudia ducked under a bunch of feathers hanging from the doorframe—to ward off evil spirits, they heard later—and found themselves temporarily blinded by the sudden gloom inside. As shapes began to take form, they realized that they were at one end of a long, broad veranda, open to the dense jungle on the left, with a continuous plywood wall on the right. Doors made of rough planking opened off the veranda every fifteen feet or so, leading to individual rooms, one for each family.

A very old lady, her matted hair framing a prunelike face, sat cross-legged at the entrance, a tiny baby in her arms. Impassively she watched them pick their way across the floor of bamboo stems, which creaked ominously with every tread. If they had not avoided large gaps in the flooring, they would have landed among the pigs and chickens underneath the house.

Out of the murky darkness three figures materialized as they approached. They were the three old men who would comprise their welcoming party, each clad in a loincloth. The middle one, apparently the headman of the longhouse, came forward and motioned Huntley and Claudia to sit with them on the floor. Huntley bowed courteously, and when they were all comfortably settled, produced a small roll of paper money.

"The *nyonya* and I would like to stay the night with you here if it is possible." He handed the bills to the headman, who glanced casually at them and nodded, tucking the cash into his waistband.

A brief discussion among the men in their own language followed and then one of the others led them to a room farther down the longhouse. Any reservations Claudia might have had about sharing a room with Huntley alone were quickly dispelled; it was quite apparent that the room was already inhabited by two people. Two old mattresses lay side by side near a Victorian dressing table adorned with bric-a-brac. Faded photographs hung on the wall, some cooking utensils lay around a pile of dead charcoal, and a half-finished carving of a crouching native occupied one corner, surrounded by chisels and wood chips. Two other mattresses were propped up against one wall; their guide implied that they were for guests.

"So far, so good," said Huntley when they were alone. "I'm hot and sticky; I don't know about you, but I feel like a swim before all the workers come in from the fields." He started rummaging in his bag for swimming trunks and towel. "You can go ahead and change. I won't peek." He turned his back on her and started peeling off his clothes.

"Okay," she said, pulling on her own bikini. She followed him out of the door. The three old men nodded solemnly at them as they made their cautious way back along the veranda.

Opposite the longhouse, the river broadened into a deep, clear pool. Smooth pebbles sparkled from the bottom, catching the shafts of sunlight that penetrated giant trees interwoven overhead. Lianas thick as a man's arm hung down from branches forty feet above.

In the pool Huntley, looking boyish and carefree without his glasses, splashed, swam, and laughed with Claudia. The water was deliciously cool, and the lethargy that had crept over them both since arriving in this steaming jungle soon evaporated.

"I have an idea!" Huntley suddenly cried, and went running up the bank of the pool carrying with him a huge liana that had almost reached the surface of the water. He hauled it ashore and then up onto a great smooth boulder with a projection at the top out over the pool.

Gripping the liana in both hands, he swung out over the water, issuing a cry like the whoop of an excited monkey. His body skimmed across the river, nearly reaching the undergrowth on the far bank. Then it swung back again and he landed neatly upright on the boulder. Claudia exploded with laughter.

"Let me have a try," she called back and scrambled out of the pool to join him on the high rock. But he took off again just as she reached him, another wild cry echoing among the tree trunks. He sounded so much like a monkey that Claudia was reminded of the *kecak* dance and sat cross-legged facing him, her arms stretched upward, swaying sideways in time to the "ch-ch" noise the dancers had made.

Now Huntley swung back and she stood up, holding a hand out to help him land. But he placed both feet on the boulder, and instead of coming to rest, swept an arm around Claudia's waist and pushed off with his feet, holding the liana with only one hand. Despite her surprise, the heavenly feeling of being held in his strong arm against his chest obliterated all other thoughts from her mind.

He deposited her safely back on the rock, from which she watched him happily swinging back and forth like a child on a garden swing. Huge blue butterflies danced through the air; kingfishers with flashing scarlet plumes darted across the water; and in the distance the chattering of monkeys mingled with the deep-throated croak of bullfrogs.

Finally Huntley tired of his swinging. Panting from exertion, he led her by the hand back down into the pool. Together, lying on their backs and still holding hands, they floated with the gentle current of the stream, watching the crisscross pattern of leaves and sky slip past as in a continuous kaleidoscope, until they felt their spines rubbing on the flat rocks in the shallows, and had to wade back up again to the deeper part. Claudia felt cool, refreshed, no longer in the least fearful of her environment, and more than ever in love with her handsome escort.

Back in their room, they each put on clean clothes, dressing wordlessly with their backs to each other. Huntley carefully combed his dark hair back into place, and when he had finished with the mirror, a small cracked one above the dressing table, Claudia brushed hers straight back in a schoolgirlish style that suited her mood, and let the back hang down in a ponytail, secured with a rubber band.

The sound of voices and weary footsteps came from outside, and a moment later the young couple whose room they had been allotted came in, bent almost double under the weight of enormous sacks of rice.

These they lowered to the ground and gravely shook hands with Huntley and Claudia.

"Good day," said the man, a squat, flat-faced youth with two-inch oval holes in his ear lobes where his mother had hung weights when he was a baby. "My name Jemeca. This my wife, Mary. We get married Singapore."

"Good day," said Claudia. "My name Claudia. This my husband, Huntley. We get married America." Somehow she managed to keep a straight face; showing no surprise, Huntley nodded in confirmation.

"Ah . . . America. Very long way." Jemeca smiled knowingly, while Mary disappeared behind a palm-leaf screen. Although topless when she had come in from the fields, she emerged later in a simple ankle-length wraparound skirt and a cotton shirt, immediately proceeding to cook their dinner. Soon the smoke from her charcoal fire was finding its way lazily up toward a hole in the roof, and she had several pans of food—pork, rice, and a vegetable like Swiss chard—steaming away nicely.

While the food was cooking, Mary got out a ladder and heaved the sacks of newly gathered rice up into the rafters above their room. Jemeca made no effort to help her, but settled down to chip away at his carving and make small talk with his guests. Mary never spoke a word; she served the other three their dinner, and then took her own behind the screen to eat it. She obviously knew her role and social standing in the household.

After the meal Jemeca took Claudia and Huntley out onto the veranda, which served as a communal gathering place. Women stood around in groups chatting; children ran helter-skelter chasing each other the length of the building; and the men began to congregate around the three elders who had first greeted the visitors.

Lanterns had been lit and hung from the rafters, casting bizarre shadows. Huntley nudged Claudia and pointed to a half-dozen smooth round objects hanging from a crossbeam above their heads. Although blackened with age, there was no doubt that they were human skulls. Claudia shivered and took Huntley's arm. They passed on quickly, but a fatal fascination kept her eyes roaming the ceiling for more evidence of head-hunting. She saw them, hanging in clusters, looking as innocent as Christmas decorations.

When they reached the group of men, the ancient headman invited them to sit by him, indicating to the dozen or so stalwarts who surrounded him that they should make room in the circle for their guests. Huntley judged this to be the moment to produce his gifts —someone had told him about the necessary ritual— and from his bag he brought out six bottles of beer and several packages of candy.

His choice was not only familiar but popular. As if by magic small glasses appeared, one for each man, and the headman poured an equal amount into each glass before distributing them. The men drank their portions down thirstily. The appearance of candy immediately brought all the children into the center of the circle; with much care the headman allocated to each child exactly the same number of jelly beans, exactly the same number of toffees.

Claudia felt strange sitting with a group of men, but she would have felt odder if custom had required her to join the women who stood around behind the circle, listening and watching but not speaking, sternly keeping quiet the now-satisfied children who chewed and sucked around their skirts.

Then Huntley introduced the topic that had inspired his visit. "You like to have visitors from other lands to your longhouse?" he asked the headman.

The wizened old head, gruesomely reminiscent of the skinless ones suspended above him, nodded. "Yes, it is a tradition of our people to make hospitality to foreigners."

"It is an additional means of livelihood for us," added a muscular young man with barely a trace of accent. "If we had more, we would not have to work the rice fields."

A murmur of approval went around the women behind them, but the men didn't seem to agree, as there was shocked head shaking and tongue clicking. One man spat the red betel nut he had been chewing onto the floor. Everyone waited respectfully for the headman to voice his opinion.

"That is my eldest son, Serapi," the chief explained to Huntley. "He has been away in Singapore, where the people live without planting rice, and he thinks that we should do the same. But the Iban have always planted rice and peppers and kept pigs and chickens. This way we are free; we do not depend on other people to live. I think our way is better."

"I could make it very easy for you to have more foreign visitors, if that was what you wanted," said Huntley. "We come from a company that builds hotels all over the world . . ."

"Mr. Hilton or Mr. Holiday Inn?" inquired the headman's son, Serapi.

"Neither, but our company is just as big. Malibu Hotels owns the Singapore Stamford. You probably know it."

"Oh, yes," said Serapi. "Very good hotel."

"Well, we have been sent by Malibu Hotels to talk

158

to you about building a hotel right here on the Skrang River."

Excited talk broke out both in the circle and among the women outside it. Those who couldn't understand English demanded a translation from those who could; everybody expressed their views on the matter at the same time. It seemed to Claudia that while a few of the younger men welcomed the prospect, the majority were opposed to it. The women were agog with excitement.

The headman subdued the hubbub with a gnarled and vein-crossed hand. "A hotel here on the river would change our way of life," he said, shaking his head sadly. "We would live as in a cage, being observed as if we were captive animals, not sharing with visitors as equals anymore. As long as our guests have to travel a whole day to reach us, they treat our longhouses as welcome resting places, and we do not have too many people coming. But if there were a new hotel just across there"—he gestured toward the river—"we would be exposed, exposed to the world forever."

General assent followed the old man's words, but Serapi was intent on having his views heard also. "But think, Father, of the work that the hotel would provide for us. Every family among us would become rich. The tourists would pay just to see our longhouse."

"There's more to life than riches," Claudia put in, and everybody turned to see her speak, so rare was it for a woman's voice to be heard in public. "Your headman is right; a hotel here would ruin your way of life. You would become richer but more unhappy."

Serapi glared at her with fire in his eyes. Restraining himself with difficulty from making some insulting reference to her sex, he asked her in a quivering voice whether she would be happy working all day in a rice paddy, and then added in a puzzled tone, "But I thought you came from the hotel company. Don't you *want* to put up a hotel here?"

Huntley answered for her. "We neither want to, nor do we not want to. We are simply exploring the possibility. If we think the hotel would be successful, we will recommend it, but if we think it would not attract many visitors, we will speak against it. Of one thing there is no doubt: The hotel would not succeed without the cooperation of the Iban, and their willingness to open their longhouses to all the visitors who come."

"Serapi," asked Claudia, "why didn't you stay in Singapore instead of coming back here if you so much prefer that kind of life?"

Serapi's chin stuck up in the air. "Because I will be the next headman of this longhouse after my father, and I want to lead my people into civilization. With a hotel here, we could have electricity and bathrooms and . . ."

"Just a minute," Huntley broke in. "If you install all those kinds of things into your longhouses, they will cease to be attractive to the vistors from outside. It's the . . . er . . . simple life you lead here that we all find so charming. If you change that, the hotel will fail."

"Sir, please," pleaded Serapi. "Don't change your mind about the hotel. Don't listen to your lady friend. Don't even listen to my father"—a gasp of horror went up from the assembled crowd—"I mean, not over something that will probably not happen in his time. But it will happen in my time as headman, and I can assure you that I will give you all the support you require to make your hotel a success. You will pay the money to me and I will see that my people do as you want. We will just sit here all day for your tourists to see."

A hush of awed silence was broken by the old headman's tired voice. "Serapi, you are still young and headstrong. Remember that as headman of this longhouse you will have responsibility to the families who live here as well as power over them."

"I know, Father," said Serapi in a humbler tone. "I think my responsibility lies in bringing them into the twentieth century. Few of them have ever seen what it is like. I have, in Singapore, and Singapore is very different from when you visited it many years ago. Here at last is our chance to develop and become rich."

"But what would be the point of having a lot of money," Claudia argued, "if to satisfy the hotel guests you had to go on living in just the same way as you are now? Your people would have gained nothing."

"Woman," growled Serapi through clenched teeth. "You keep out of this. Leave the decision to the gentleman here with you, if you please."

"Oh, no, we will make the decision together," said Huntley. "She is just as important as me on this mission."

"In that case I will have to see that she doesn't influence you too much," said Serapi, an evil smile turning up the corners of his mouth.

Claudia looked at Huntley hopelessly and shrugged. It was most unfortunate that electric tension had developed as a result of Huntley's tentative feelers on the subject of a Skrang River hotel, but no doubt the fanatical Serapi would be put in his place by his father and the other longhouse men as soon as the visitors left tomorrow. Claudia felt convinced that the Iban were not yet ready for a hotel in their midst. She suspected that Huntley felt the same.

The arrival of three musicians heralded dancing.

The instruments were a crude, mournful-sounding xylophone, a gong, and a bongo drum. Four dancers appeared. Two were male; they wore ceremonial plumed headdresses and brandished in their right hands long curved swords from scabbards around their waists, protecting themselves from their mock opponent with bamboo shields in their left. They writhed and jumped to the wailing music, issuing war cries as they struck fiercely at each other with their swords. The two girls just stood there, as immobile as show girls in a nightclub. As a relic of the Iban's days of tribal battles, the dance was interesting but it had none of the polish and formal choreography of the Balinese dances.

The programmed part of the entertainment was now over, and the evening became amateur night. First the headman himself, amid cheers, belted on a sword and leaped into his own version of the war dance, twisting and squirming with remarkable agility. Then the other two old men went through a few minutes of slow gyrations before retiring to polite applause.

Serapi leaped to his feet. He handed one long scimitar to his brother and took the other himself. "Let you and me show these people how we used to do battle in the old days."

Moving slowly at first in the manner of the previous dancers, the brothers sparred around the ring of spectators like two boxers testing each other's strength. Then Serapi signaled to the musicians to speed up the tempo, and he began to slash more fiercely at his opponent's sword. With the repeated thrusts and parries the event took on more the aspect of a fencing match, but without armor or masks. Serapi managed to sneak past his brother's defenses enough to inflict a tiny scratch on the other's chest. At the sight of the drop of blood, he let out a provocative yell, goading his adversary to take his revenge.

The younger man's temper plainly flared as he began slashing wildly with his weapon. But Serapi warded off each blow as it came. Again and again the clash of steel fused with the now hectic tempo of the music. Serapi backed away from the onslaught, moving around the circle, almost treading on the feet of the audience. He retreated past his father, who seemed mesmerized by the performance, and was exactly opposite Claudia when he bellowed and arched his back, holding up his protective sword, inviting his brother to smite it with all his strength. Then, as the mighty blow descended, Serapi whipped his sword out of the way and ducked sideways. The steel blade now had a clear path to Claudia's neck . . .

She felt her head wrenched back as Huntley seized her ponytail and dragged it to the floor. The blade flashed past above her and stuck deep into the wall behind, quivering with a metallic twang. The young warrior, lunging forward against no resistance without Serapi's sword to check him, collapsed in a heap beside her. A horrified expression came over his dazed features—horror at what he had so nearly done, led into treachery by his own brother, Serapi.

Pandemonium broke loose. Huntley pulled Claudia to her feet, the old headman helping on the other side. The women outside the circle were screaming and hiding their heads in their hands, but the men had seen exactly what had happened and had converged on Serapi, pinning his arms behind his back and dragging him forward to face his father.

The frail old chief fixed his powerful firstborn with a stare that would shrivel anyone less defiant than his son, who glared back at him, unrepentant. A few words passed between them in their native tongue, and then, at an order from the chief, the other men roughly manhandled Serapi away down the veranda. He went, sullenly, not struggling, and at the same time the women and children slunk away to their rooms until only Huntley and Claudia were left with the headman.

"I have no words to say how sorry I am. Serapi has always had a thirst for revenge, and you, young lady, brought out the worst in him tonight. And to use his brother's sword for the purpose instead of his own, that makes his attempt to behead you even more dastardly."

"It . . . it's all right," said Claudia, controlling her tears and massaging the muscles of her neck where Huntley's lifesaving jerk had wrenched them. "My friend here was in time to see that no harm came to me."

"I was almost expecting it," said Huntley. "I could see from his expression earlier on that he wasn't going to let Claudia spoil his dream if he could help it."

"It won't be Serapi's choice now," said the headman with a tinge of sadness in his voice. "He is my eldest, but I do not have to appoint him to succeed me. Now of course I will not. And what is more, I will have to think of a suitable punishment for attempting to kill one of our treasured guests. Please do not mention this incident in Kuching unless you feel you have to notify the Malaysian police," the watery eyes pleaded. "It would be the end of our tourist trade if you do."

"We can't tell the police because we're in this country illegally from Indonesia," said Huntley. "So please don't tell them we came."

"That is settled, then. I will deal with my son myself. And I will wish you a good night, safe from the evil spirits." The old man hobbled off.

CHAPTER TEN

Near silence had desecnded on the veranda, which only a few minutes before had been the setting for dancing and revelry. Huntley suggested that they wait a while before going to bed.

Claudia agreed. "I'm still a bit too shaken up to be able to sleep. When I think how near I came to being killed . . ."

"There's more than a touch of savagery lurking in these people yet," said Huntley, slipping a comforting arm around her waist. "It's ironic that it should come out in Serapi, because he's the one who has been exposed to more of the civilizing influence of a big city like Singapore than any of the others."

"You know what they say about the asphalt jungle. I never feel safe in Pittsburgh or even in Philly. The woods out there somehow seem safer, while in fact they are probably full of dangerous animals."

"Actually they're not. The only man-killing creature left in Borneo is the wild boar, and there are very few of those. Up until the hunters made them extinct, rhinos used to live all through here, but not anymore. It's all quite safe."

"Let's go for a walk by the river, then," Claudia suggested. "I feel like getting away from this place for a little while, and it looks pretty down there in the moonlight."

"Okay. I'll try and take your mind off what happened."

She smiled up at him, although all that she could see of his face was a silhouette of his long nose and chin and hair flopping over his brow.

Hand in hand they made their way down the ladder from the longhouse and then followed the path down to the water's edge. Being already barefoot, they naturally waded into the river. Tiny wavelets gurgled and sparkled in the silver glow that twinkled through gaps in the enormous trees.

Claudia stuck her thumb through the back of Huntley's belt; his hand around her chest held her closely to him. Wandering upstream over the smooth flat stones, their ankles parting the shallow water with each step, the horror of an hour ago gradually ebbed. Claudia found herself becoming more and more conscious of Huntley's nearness, as though their thoughts were following the same route as their bodies.

By some sort of unspoken mutual consent, they both came to a halt at the same moment and turned to face each other. Huntley's other hand joined the first in pressing her to him. Eagerly she craned her neck up to meet his face, ignoring the pain in her muscles. For a long moment he studied her hair, her broad cheekbones, her eyes, her daintily tilted nose, and finally, when her lips parted, he pressed his own mouth down upon them, softly at first, but then with growing ardor.

At last he drew his head away. He smoothed her hair, the hair he had had to pull to save her life, with his gentle fingers. She closed her eyes and began to feel the world slipping away under the spell of his hypnotic touch. She had never felt so much at oneness with a man; she wanted the feeling to last forever.

"Are you less distressed now?" he asked tenderly.

a hot glint flashing in his eyes, a glint of pure desire.

She nodded, knowing from the lump in her throat that, if she spoke, the words would come out brokenly. How she longed to confess her love to him! Out here, the Bali Breezes Hotel seemed an eternity away, and Huntley no longer the stern manager. Out here it wouldn't matter if she said the words "I love you," words that pounded through her brain to the exclusion of all else. Yet she somehow managed to keep silent.

This time she knew for sure that he had kissed her for herself alone; news of this kiss would never reach the ears of the hotel staff. His embrace had kindled in her an all-consuming passion, a need for greater intimacy—now while his fire still burned brightly, as she could sense it did. Who would know if they spent this night as a stolen night of love? What difference would it make on their return? Instinctively she quickened their dawdling pace back up the path to the longhouse.

But, alas, an Iban dwelling on the Skrang River in Borneo is not exactly conducive to lovemaking if you are a Westerner accustomed to clean sheets, soft carpets, gentle fragrances, and privacy. Back in Jemeca's room, the bamboo floor squeaked and moved under her feet, the bare mattresses not at all beckoning, cooking odors mingled with must and sweat, and Jemeca himself snoring so loudly that the dust shook off the rafters. And so the devil in Claudia remained outside the room.

Slipping into a pair of loose pajamas, she stretched out on the mattress in a mood for nothing more than sleep, and by the time Huntley had doused the lantern across the room a few minutes later, unconsciousness had overtaken her, and she slept soundly until her watch said eight o'clock.

By that time Jemeca, his wife, and all the able-bodied inhabitants of the longhouse had gone off to the fields to work—all except Serapi. He was to remain in leg irons under guard in his room until the guests had departed and his temper had cooled to the point where his father could deal with him.

"I must ask you now, *tuan*," said the headman, "what are you going to do about your hotel? Will you build it in spite of us?"

"We haven't discussed it between ourselves yet," Huntley answered, "but I'm personally inclined to think we should drop the idea. We might run some tours here from our hotels in Singapore and Bali, so you can expect to have more visitors than the ones you now receive from Kuching, and that will bring in a little more money for you, as we will pay well for your hospitality . . ."

The headman bowed his head and patted his waist-band gratefully. "That would be generous of you."

"But that is as far as I feel we should go at present."

It took only a few minutes for Huntley and Claudia to repack their small bags, and by nine o'clock the helicopter was airborne once more. Claudia could hardly believe that in the last twenty-four hours she had lived the primitive life of a remote jungle tribe with all its attendant pleasures as well as its discomforts, that she had also been saved from a vicious murder, and that the man she loved had shown how he felt about her, if only physically, and probably temporarily.

Undoubtedly he felt the same way about Negara when it came to sex, but unfortunately his admiration for the tall, slim Javanese went beyond that. And now Negara, disappointed by Wilbur, was waiting at the hotel ready to turn on all the heat she could muster as soon as Huntley returned. Claudia's own role was the humiliating one of protecting the man from damaging gossip until he deemed the time ripe for making it public. After last night, every moment she spent with Huntley would be a bittersweet pleasure, and every occasion when she took his arm or danced close to him or gazed longingly into his eyes would be a ghastly sham. She dreaded the resumption of life at Bali Breezes. As much as anything, she dreaded the need to keep Huntley thinking she liked Anton, for that meant acquiescing to Anton's flamboyant attentions when she couldn't care less if she ever saw the recreational director again.

Huntley must have read her mind, because he turned to her as soon as he was satisfied that their course for Bali had been set and said, "You'll be anxious to get back to the company of Anton Reinholtz again."

"Yes, but I've enjoyed this trip too, if one forgets that flashing knife blade. Did I ever really thank you for saving my life?"

"Indeed you did," he said, his eyes not moving from the dials on the instrument panel. "By letting me kiss you the way you did. Under the circumstances it must have been hard for you to bear with me. But we had just been through a somewhat emotional experience, so I hope you'll accept my forwardness as no more than a release of tension."

"Of course. I felt the same way about it."

"Good. So we can dismiss the whole incident, can we?"

"That would probably be best," she said, her heart curling up at the sound of her own words. They didn't speak to each other again, except for trivialities, until they were safely on the ground at Bali Breezes.

Huntley addressed her once more in his formal manager's voice and looked at her with a thoughtful expression of cold appraisal as he spoke. "This afternoon I'll write out my report for Uncle Wilbur on the

Skrang River project. I think I can incorporate your views satisfactorily, but I'd like you to see the document and be there when I present it. Come up to my office at about six, will you?"

"Sure, that'd be fine," Claudia replied. "We'll be through by seven, won't we?"

"I see no reason why not. Why, do you have an assignation?"

"Today's Saturday, and Penebel does her first performance of the *barong* and *kris* dance at the buffet supper tonight. I'm sure you won't want to miss that either."

In her room Claudia thankfully stripped off her jeans and T-shirt, stuffing them with her underwear straight into the laundry bag, dust, and all. Next she soaked herself in the bathtub and thoroughly washed her hair. She wanted to rid herself of all the clinging dirt and smells of the longhouse. At last, her head wrapped in a towel and cool in her dressing room in air-conditioned luxury, she lay on her bed and rested from the exertion of her adventure. Lazily she thought of Huntley, probably already at work on his report and other duties, and shook her head sadly at the unfairness of it all. The grind of his job was unfair to Huntley, and the playacting she was forced to endure was unfair to her. Yet she knew her duty to Huntley as well as he knew his to the hotel.

Fully recuperated by six o'clock, she presented herself at the manager's office, clean and crisp in pastel linen slacks and a white blouse, her hair shining and neatly pinned up. Huntley was behind his desk, back in uniform and thick-rimmed glasses, shaven, and scrubbed.

"Sit down and read through this, Claudia. If you don't mind, don't say anything until you've finished it, because I don't want to be interrupted in what I'm doing here." He gave her a three-page typed report entitled, "Malibu Hotels Ltd. Confidential Report on Expediency of Establishing Unit at Skrang River, Borneo." It gave a concise account of the location, the longhouse, and the life-style of the Iban tribesmen, ending with the recommendation that the matter be dropped for at least another ten years, but in the meanwhile, contact be maintained by running tours there from Singapore to Bali.

She finished reading and then sat quietly with the report on her lap until he put his pen down and looked up, pushing aside the usual stray lock of hair. "Well, what do you think of it?"

"I think it covers the situation fine. I guess you didn't feel like mentioning the risks involved. Risks of murder, I mean."

"No, I thought the directors in California would think I was exaggerating. Either that or they would regard the whole thing as an exotic tourist attraction and go ahead and build it anyway."

"Are the directors as stupid as all that?" laughed Claudia.

A harsh voice from behind her said, "Was that you telling this girl the Malibu directors are stupid, Huntley?" Wilbur Fox had slipped through the door, his footsteps muffled by the thick pile carpet.

"I never said any such thing," replied Huntley in the clipped tone he reserved for conversation with his uncle. "Here's your report on the Skrang River unit. Claudia agrees with it."

"Whassit say? I left my glasses someplace." Wilbur lowered his bulk into a chair.

"We don't recommend building there. It's too far in the wilds, and the headhunters are pretty tame anyway. No future in the idea."

"I guessed as much," said Wilbur. "The guy who told

me about it seemed a bit of a crackpot to me. But send a copy to San Francisco for them to keep on file."

"If you're looking for somewhere to put up a new hotel, why don't you try Kuta Beach on the other side of this island?" Claudia put in. "It's got a lovely beach and there aren't any big hotels like this."

"We'd thought of that, young lady," said Wilbur, puffing on his cigar. "But I'd pretty well decided to expand this place instead. We have an option on the property to the east of us."

Claudia remembered that this was the land that Huntley had pointed out to her when they went for a walk that evening last week. He was against the plan because it would disrupt the lives of the fishermen and their families. She must try to dissuade Wilbur from it.

"I've heard lots of the guests say Bali Breezes is too big as it is. Big hotels get too impersonal, they say." It wasn't exactly true that she had heard it here, but it was a general opinion that she had heard expressed elsewhere.

"Izzat so?" Wilbur sounded interested. "Waal, the trend is toward smaller, more intimate places these days, that's for sure."

"And the land at Kuta would be much cheaper," Claudia persisted. "Have you been down there, Mr. Fox?"

"No, I can't say I have."

"Why not let me take you to Kuta tomorrow? I know it well as I used to live in a guesthouse there before I came to work here."

"I don't as a rule turn down offers from pretty young girls to take me around places," smirked Wilbur. "Okay, I'll call you tomorrow when I'm ready to go."

Huntley coughed. "I think it's an excellent suggestion. In fact, I think I'll come along with you. Another

Malibu Hotel on this island would implicate me a good deal."

"There's no need for that, Huntley. You've got your work cut out here. Claudia and I will be quite all right by ourselves, won't we?"

"Of course, Mr. Fox. You don't need to come, Huntley."

"Well, I don't know . . ." said Huntley dubiously.

"If you'll excuse me, I must go and change now. Penebel's first performance is tonight." She got up to go.

"Oh . . . er, Claudia." Huntley had risen from his desk too, and in that moment of facing each other Claudia was amazed to see a flicker of desire in his eyes, the same as after his kiss last night.

"Yes?" She almost whispered it.

"Would you watch the show with me tonight? I'd appreciate your opinion of Penebel's interpretation of the *dewi* role."

Ideas raced through Claudia's brain. What on earth was happening? Here was Wilbur agreeing to go for a drive with her tomorrow right after he had given Negara the thumbs down, and now Huntley, who hadn't seen Negara for two days, was inviting her to the performance tonight. Or was this part of her decoy role? Then what was the meaning of that look in his eyes? Meanwhile, she was supposed to be keen on Anton, wasn't she? The situation was decidedly tricky.

"I'm sorry," she smiled sweetly at Huntley, "but I already have plans to watch the show with someone else."

"Anton Reinholtz?"

"Yes, as a matter of fact. He . . ."

"I see." The response was curt. "You better go, then."

Claudia dived for the door to cover her confusion

173

as well as her wretchedness at having to bring Huntley's cold disdain upon her own head.

The next thing was to seek out Anton and persuade him to take her to the buffet; it shouldn't be hard.

She found him in the gymnasium practicing weight lifting. "That was two-hundred thirty pounds in the snatch," he said proudly, lowering a huge barbell to the floor. "Ten pounds better than last week."

"That's great," said Claudia a little wearily. "By the way, do you know there's a new dancer performing at the buffet supper tonight?"

"I heard that," Anton replied, making his biceps stand out to be admired. "I intend to see her."

Claudia's heart drooped. Anton had another date!

"Oh, Anton," she cooed. "I do so want to see Penebel too, and I just hate to sit alone. Would you mind terribly if I joined you?"

"It is no difference," he shrugged. "Hilda, she insisted that her mother be with us, so why not you also?"

"You're going with the Steiners?" said Claudia with marked relief. "Oh, that's marvelous. Then I won't be a bit in the way." Better still, Huntley would understand.

The *barong* and *kris* dance was a joy to behold. The *barong*, acted by two men the way a stage horse is presented, was truly magnificent with his ruff, beard and gnashing wooden teeth up front, while his thick hair trailed on the ground at the back, surmounted by an ornamental saddle and a waving plume for a tail. His friend the white-faced monkey provided comic relief as the *barong* fought off three attackers during the first scene. It wasn't until the second act that Penebel made her appearance, dancing with breathtaking precision to the beautiful harmony of the *gamelan* orchestra. Claudia could hardly take her eyes off the gorgeous, lilting figure on the stage, but from time to time she stole a glance at where Huntley was sitting with Negara. He looked enthralled; she thoroughly bored.

At the end, out came the dozen *kris* dancers, each wielding his curved dagger or *kris*. Unable to defeat the evil spirit Rangda and thus save the *dewi*'s beloved son, they stabbed themselves to death, but the *dewi*, enacting marvelously tender pathos in her movements, made her sacrifice for her son, and the dancers magically recovered in the finale.

Huntley rose and left immediately, looking neither to right nor left, with Negara in hot pursuit. Claudia said good night to Anton and Hilda. Frau Steiner announced that she was going to bed too. The young couple made little attempt to disguise their relief at being left alone.

At the elevator Frau Steiner said to Claudia, "A very handsome young man that is which you introduced to Hilda. He is a good man too, you think?"

"Oh, absolutely," replied Claudia, feeling there was nothing to be gained by worrying Hilda's mother. "He's completely reliable." Yes, she thought, Anton could always be relied upon to switch his attentions to the next strapping young goddess to swim into his ken. It made her own sacrificial role easier to bear.

Wilbur's summons to Claudia for the trip to Kuta Beach came shortly after ten o'clock the next morning. "All right, Wilbur, I'll see you downstairs in half an hour," she said.

"*You're* going after the old ram now?" Negara asked incredulously. "Honey, you're wasting your time."

Claudia laughed. "No, this is just a business thing. He wants to look around Kuta and I happen to know it quite well. What time did you come in last night? You must have been very quiet."

"Ridiculously early," the dancer replied, yawning and stretching her long lithe body like a cat might. "Poor old Huntley! He said he hadn't slept much the night before at that place in Borneo you went to. I gather it was pretty uncomfortable."

"It was," Claudia agreed. "I certainly was ready for bed right after the dance last night; I'm not surprised that he was too."

"One drink and then, 'Off you go to bed, Negara,' with a little peck on the cheek. Ah, well, there'll be other nights."

Claudia turned away, unable to comment.

Wilbur was more impressed with the village of Kuta, and particularly with its endless stretch of broad yellow sand, than he had expected to be, he said. His developer's eye spotted an area of delapidated native shacks scattered through a grove of palm trees right on the seashore. If that property was for sale cheap, he said, it might do very well for a hotel. And that, thought Claudia in triumph, means no expansion of Bali Breezes!

In the afternoon Eleanor Davis rang down from the manager's office to tell her that her presence was required.

"Come in, Claudia," said Huntley as soon as she set foot on the soft floor of his office. "I thought I'd just let you know how well you handled my difficult uncle this morning. He came back from your jaunt to Kuta all fired up about a piece of beach property he saw. If he can pick it up at a reasonable price, he plans to pass up his option on the land next to Bali Breezes."

"So your friends in the village won't be disturbed?"

"That's right. I'm delighted about that. What's more, he has gone off to Australia without ramming down my throat any of the other changes that I was against."

"Good. He didn't take Negara with him either."

Huntley smiled and looked surprised. "So you thought he might do that too, did you? I must say it had crossed my mind. Thank goodness he didn't—we really need her here."

"Even since we discovered Penebel?"

Huntley hesitated a moment, as if having difficulty choosing his words. "Yes, Penebel is very good—I enjoyed her as the *dewi* last night—but she hasn't got the statuesque figure Negara has, the show-girl professionalism that our sophisticated audiences prefer. It's a matter of class, I suppose."

Claudia could think of no suitable reply. There was no point in arguing with him about the two dancers' relative merits; no amount of discussion would ever change his mind—not as long as he kept Negara on the pedestal he liked to worship at.

"I'm sorry I couldn't accept your invitation last night," she said. "But as you probably saw, I did have a duty to perform."

"Yes, I was glad to see you were with the Steiners. From what you said, I thought you had a private date with Reinholtz."

"You mustn't jump to conclusions," she smiled. "I'm free this evening if you'd like to take me to dinner."

"I'd like to very much, Claudia. I suppose it would be all right. From the staff's point of view, I mean."

"You took Negara last night and that was all right."

"Oh, that was so that we could talk about Penebel's act. It would seem quite natural for me to be watching the new dancer with the old one."

"I see," said Claudia. "Well, perhaps over dinner tonight we could be discussing my future role, if any, in Bali Breezes."

And indeed Huntley did start the evening by discussing her job. They had been served a Javanese curry that was one of Chef Rekans's specialties, and

Claudia was putting out the fire in her mouth with a swallow of beer, when Huntley sprang on her the news that she would be moving tomorrow into the room vacated by Wilbur Fox. "It'll be nice for you to have your own room. You and Negara have both been very good about sharing, but this morning she absolutely insisted that she get her room back to herself."

Claudia couldn't restrain herself this time. "You don't think that Wilbur's departure without Negara might have anything to do with Negara's demand for a room to herself?"

Huntley frowned slightly. "No, I don't. How could it?"

"Well . . ." Claudia began to wish she had kept her mouth shut.

"Tell me, I don't understand."

"The room we share is just one of the regular hotel rooms. It's not like your bedroom, where any visitor emerging in the morning would be seen by all your staff. It's private. That's why Negara wants it to herself."

Huntley shook his head. "I'm sorry, Claudia, I don't see what you're driving at. If it's anything to do with Negara's personal habits, who she was visiting last week, that sort of thing, I don't think it's any business of yours—or mine for that matter. So let's change the subject. Have you heard about the Balinese magic *kris*?"

Claudia sighed. If he didn't understand that, he must be blind. "Magic *kris*?" she said wearily, "No, what's that?"

"There are thought to be three of them, originally made by the gods. Whoever owns one cannot be killed. President Sukarno of Indonesia had one. He survived many assassination attempts, some quite incredibly."

"Very interesting," said Claudia, her mind on other

things. "You still haven't told me what my work here is to be now that the Germans have left."

"I haven't, have I," Huntley nodded, licking his lips over the last of the curry. "I'd really like you to go on doing what you did for the Germans. We get a number of VIPs coming through here, and it does help to have someone to entertain their wives in their own language."

"I suppose I could try and brush up the French I learned in school . . ."

"That wouldn't be worth it. We hardly ever get any important French people at Bali Breezes. No, the people we're getting more and more of are the Japanese. And their wives never seem to speak English. The next group is due in about a week. So you'd have plenty of time to learn some basic Japanese before they come . . ."

Claudia put down her fork and stared at him. "You've got to be kidding! Me learn Japanese in a week? Why, it doesn't even have the same letters as we do!"

"I wouldn't expect you to be fluent right away. And the speaking would be more important than the writing. I could find you a Japanese teacher in Denpasar, and if you studied twelve or fifteen hours a day, you should be able to carry on simple conversations in a week. Meanwhile, get a book from the library."

"And that's what you want me to do?" Claudia said sadly. "Well, I suppose I could try . . ." But it seemed like an awfully tall order, and how could she face his disappointment in her if she failed miserably?

"I'll get onto a teacher for you tomorrow," he said cheerfully. "Let me know in a few days how you're getting on. Now, if you've finished your dinner, I must get back to the office."

Politely, he held her chair for her as she rose from the table, and then, smiling, courteously stood back to let her out of the dining-room door first.

Huntley's attention was not on Claudia once they were outside. "Well, good night now. I enjoyed dining with you." He turned abruptly toward the back staircase that led to the management suite, leaving her standing, lonely and worried, in the middle of the lobby. The change in his behavior—solicitous in the public dining room but rudely dismissing her as soon as they were outside—brought back all her awful doubts about his motives for employing her.

Her distress was not alleviated after half an hour spent the next morning with a book called *The Fundamentals of Japanese Conversation.* There was nothing remotely familiar about any of it. She tried practicing a few of the weird sounds described in the book as basic Japanese vowels, and then threw it down in disgust and started packing her clothes to move to the fourteenth floor.

Her suitcase was almost full when Negara burst into the room. As usual, Claudia had been asleep before she came in last night, and had departed for the library before Negara woke up.

The dancer slammed the door behind her and stood with her back to it, glaring at Claudia. "Packing to move upstairs, are you?"

Claudia stared back, shattered by the angry tone. "Yes, but . . ."

"You're not intending to lure our esteemed manager into your little private nest up there, I hope."

"Of course not. What's the matter, Negara?"

"I saw you last night, billing and cooing over the dinner table, while I had to eat by myself in the corner—that's what's the matter! I'm warning you,

Claudia, here and now, it's hands off Huntley Fox for you; otherwise there'll be open war between us."

"What the hell are you talking about?" Claudia's temper was rising too. "I know you've been thrown over by Wilbur, and now you're working on Huntley as second choice, but that's got nothing to do with me. Last week you encouraged me to be seen with the manager, so if he invites me to dinner I'm going to accept. And that goes for anything else he has in mind . . ."

"Where did he take you last night after dinner?"

"If you'd thought to look in here, you'd have found me fast asleep by nine thirty. And him working at his desk. Alone, unfortunately."

"So!" Negara advanced slowly toward the bed where Claudia's suitcase was laid out. "You admit you would have liked him to take you somewhere after dinner. And end up in his bed, no doubt. I thought you were keen on him last week. I didn't care then, but I sure as hell care now. So lay off, understand!"

Claudia put the last of her things in her suitcase and her purse, and left the room without saying another word, leaving the door swinging open. As she stalked proudly down the red-carpeted corridor, she heard Negara slam the door behind her and snap shut the bolt.

She threw the unpacked case on the luggage rack in the room on the fourteenth floor, and lay down, fully clothed, on the bed. Lunchtime came and went. Then, in the heat of the afternoon, she put on her shorts and sandals and slipped out along the beach beyond the hotel grounds until she came to the small village where Huntley had taken her to visit on their first evening together.

Sitting on the trunk of a fallen coconut palm, she watched the crabs sidling to and fro, in and out of little holes in the sand, and recalled with a wry smile how Huntley had guided her that night, and how she had so hoped for his kiss before they parted. Now a new complication had been added to the already unhappy situation of her one-way love: an insanely jealous Negara. With Negara's talons into him, Claudia would almost have to make love to him in public if she was going to be successful in averting curious eyes from the truth, and thereby protect his name. And that would certainly give him a name of another kind, a worse one. She couldn't help him anymore. Besides, his coolness after dinner last night proved that, even after Borneo, he still had no real affection for her. Her love for him was hopeless.

The ramshackle houses of the village, the boats, the crabs, and the rough, unraked sand all made Kuta seem more attractive right now than any luxury hotel. She collected her things and caught the next *boomi* back across the island.

CHAPTER ELEVEN

Claudia's landlady took her back into the house with no questions asked. Claudia slept late the first morning, and woke drained of ambition. Eventually she dressed, strolled around the dusty streets of Kuta, and wound up on the beach. The lazy blue sea lulled her taut nerves and coaxed her mind away from the dreadful letdowns of her last day at Bali Breezes. By the time bedtime came, she had determined to resume her life and interests as if the hotel and Huntley hadn't existed.

Accordingly she took off the next afternoon in a *boomi* for Bedulu, hoping to catch Tabanan's dance school at practice. Penebel wouldn't be there of course, but the enthusiasm she had generated at the school likely carried on in her absence.

The *boomi* put her down at the edge of the village. Claudia's spirits were quite high as she picked her way along the familiar potholed track that led to Tabanan's house and the open-air theater beyond it. She waved cheerfully at naked children who darted out in front of her from the bushes and exchanged a warm smile with a marvelously erect young girl who walked assuredly along dressed in nothing but a short skirt, balancing a pitcher of water on her head. Claudia's ears strained for the first joyous rhythm of the *gamelan* orchestra, but no sound came to meet her.

At Tabanan's house she went through the mandatory ritual for visiting a Balinese in his home. She took a small pencil from her purse as a gift. Today he took her gift as correctly and graciously as usual, but the ceremony was dispensed with as quickly as was consistent with politeness; the old man seemed decidedly agitated.

"Claudia *nyonya*, I am so glad you have come. Perhaps you can tell us the meaning of the evil which has befallen our Penebel at your hotel. Now I am blaming myself for letting her go. . . ."

"What has happened?" Claudia asked anxiously. "I left the hotel two days ago, so I haven't heard anything."

"Well, it seems that a wicked spirit entered Penebel's soul. She stole some valuable jewels belonging to the dancer she replaced, the one with the injured ankle."

"Negara? Negara certainly has some nice jewelry, but what makes you think Penebel stole it?"

"She says she didn't, of course. In fact, she swore to me on the holiness of Wismu that she never did it, but the fact remains that these jewels were found in Penebel's room, and the dancer Negara has witnesses to that."

"Is Penebel here now? Has she been fired from her job?"

"No, she is still down there, working. She came up for a quick visit yesterday and told us all about it. The girl Negara agreed not to report the incident to the manager if Penebel gave her all her salary—and that includes the part that was to be paid to the school here to help with our new costumes."

"But that's blackmail!" cried Claudia. "And anyway I don't believe a word of the story of the theft. Negara could have planted her jewels in Penebel's room herself and then pretended to find them. Negara is absolutely unscrupulous . . ."

"Claudia, you know the Balinese custom about thievery. If you suspect someone of stealing something from you, you ask him to give you something. And if he does give you the something, that is an admission of guilt, and it must be done because the gods will severely punish a thief who refuses such a request. And Penebel has agreed to give this Negara all the money she will earn at Bali Breezes, so it must be she who stole the jewels." Tabanan's wrinkled old face took on an aspect of utter misery. "I am as unhappy over our Penebel's yielding to temptation as I am over the loss of our money or hers."

"But don't you see," Claudia argued. "Negara was betting that Penebel would quit rather than work for nothing. She was fearfully jealous of Penebel's success. But even though Penebel didn't quit, she had to agree to give Negara her money, because otherwise the manager would have been told and she would have been fired. And that would mean not only the loss of all her earnings, but the loss of an opportunity to make her name as a dancer as well. She wouldn't have lied to you about it, Tabanan, and certainly not have sworn by Wismu."

"Well, I did wonder about that. But this other dancer, she must know that the gods will punish her if she extorts money in this way from Penebel."

"Negara's not Balinese, not even a Hindu. She comes from Jakarta, and would simply be preying on Penebel's beliefs. I know she was furious at Penebel being hired to take her place, and this was her way of getting her revenge.'"

Tabanan's eyebrows rose. "From Jakarta, you say? Well, that does change things a bit. But, Claudia, what can we do about it? You've left the hotel yourself."

"I'm going back down there right now," said Claudia, "and I'm going to tell the manager about the whole thing." Claudia's eyes flared and her chin stuck aggressively in the air.

"But is that wise?" Tabanan was still worried. "Suppose it is true that Penebel stole the jewels; if you tell the manager, the whole world will know, and it will bring disgrace upon her and upon this school as well."

"Don't worry," said Claudia. "I have enough faith in Penebel to be quite sure she isn't guilty. And I'm going to prove it if it's the last thing I do. You'll get your money for the school; just leave it to me."

"I do so hope you're right," said Tabanan, wringing his hands now.

"I will be," replied Claudia confidently. "But I may have a hard time proving it to the manager. Unfortunately Negara can do nothing wrong in his eyes, and he'll be a bit mad with me for walking out on him, but I'll manage it somehow."

Ten minutes later Claudia was climbing into a *boomi* headed for Sanur. Already a plan was beginning to form in her mind. It depended on witnesses.

The quick tropical darkness was beginning to envelop the Bali Breezes Hotel when Claudia raised herself stiffly from the long, bumpy ride in the minibus and climbed out the back. She had decided to get Penebel's version of the story first; knowing that the little dancer had been accommodated in the staff quarters, she went there to seek her out.

The staff quarters provided rooms for most of the members of the hotel staff. It lay down a narrow track through the brush at an angle to the paved drive of the main entrance.

Boldly she walked in through the open front door and found herself in a hall furnished with old chairs and sofas. Two staircases and several passages led off in different directions. Half a dozen young boys and a couple of girls, all Balinese, lounged around, reading chatting, or drinking from Coke bottles. They didn't see Claudia come in, but when she crossed over to the two girls, they all stopped talking and watched.

"Hello," said Claudia to the two girls, whose wide coal-black eyes regarded her with suspicion. "I'm looking for Penebel. She's the dancer who moved into this building last week. Do you know which is her room?"

The girls stared at each other uncomprehendingly. Then one of the boys called out from his chair, "Who is it you are wanting, *nyonya?*"

"Ah, you speak English," Claudia smiled gratefully at him. "I'm trying to find Penebel, the dancer."

The boy's face burst into a grin. "Very good dancer,

Penebel. Best ever in hotel. I know her but she not know me. She not go with any boys in the hotel."

"You must excuse her for that," said Claudia. "She's shy and very young. Would you tell me which is her room?"

"Okay," said the youth. "Maybe if I take you to her, she remember me another day. Maybe she say yes to come swimming with me." He was taller than most young Balinese and had a nice open face with a mischievous smile that appealed to Claudia.

"I'll put in a good word for you. I think she could use a friend right now. What's your name?"

"My name Kardha. Now I take you Penebel's room." He started off up one of the staircases. "You friend of Penebel? She very beautiful."

Claudia followed the boy up the rickety stairs, turned left down a long corridor at the top and then right through a swing door halfway down it. This apparently led them into a whole new annex to the original house, because they followed two more corridors before stopping in front of a paneled wooden door. None of the doors had numbers or identification of any kind on them. Kardha must have been observing Penebel's movements carefully to know that this was her room.

Claudia knocked and a faint, frightened voice answered, "Who is it?"

"It's Claudia. You remember me, Penebel. I met you at Bedulu with Tabanan . . ."

"Tabanan!" The sound of hasty footsteps crossing a bare floor was followed by the door's being flung open. Penebel stood in a simple white blouse and dark skirt, one hand on the door handle, her feet splayed in a dancer's pose, her head cocked to one side. "Claudia. Yes, I remember you. You want to see me?" Her voice clearly betrayed her fear and doubt.

"Can I come in?" asked Claudia, at which Penebel drew back, a little reluctantly it seemed. Kardha followed Claudia in, smiling, but Penebel simply stared at him, understanding nothing.

"No, Kardha," said Claudia sternly. "I want to have a private talk with Penebel, so you'll have to go now. Penebel, this is Kardha, who works in the hotel. He is a nice boy who showed me your room; in fact I think he's an admirer of yours. Perhaps you'd like to go swimming with him some time."

A thin smile crept around Penebel's mouth. "Okay, perhaps. If you say he nice boy."

"Thank you, *nyonya*." Kardha bowed his head and backed out of the door, still giving Penebel the full blast of his engaging grin. Claudia closed the door behind him.

"Now, Penebel," she said, taking the one and only chair for herself and indicating that Penebel should sit on the bed, "Let's hear all about this business of Negara's jewelry."

Penebel's hand flew to her mouth. "You know about that? The manager, he know too?"

"No, no, it's all right. Nobody knows except me. Tabanan told me about it this afternoon, so I came straight down here to find out for myself. Now, tell me straight, Penebel, did you or did you not take Negara's jewels?"

The dancer's big soulful eyes clouded with tears, and she shook her head vehemently. "No, *nyonya*, I promise you . . . I swear to you . . ."

"All right, dear, I believe you," said Claudia, getting up to put an arm around the girl's shoulder to console her. "Now suppose you tell me exactly what happened." She composed herself on the chair to listen.

"It was two days ago, at about this time. I was here in my room resting, and in comes this Negara—you know her—and with her is this man, a big strong man. They not knock or anything, just come in, and she says to me, 'Where are my jewels, you thief?' or something like that. I say I not know what she is talking about, so she tell me I am a liar and she start searching the room, throwing everything around. I real frightened, because I not understand. Then suddenly this Negara, she get the man to help her lift up my mattress, and there underneath is a little scarf. She take the scarf and shake it, and out come all these precious things I never even seen before!" Penebel was on the verge of tears again, but responded to another of Claudia's reassuring hugs.

"All right, what happened after that?"

"Well, she say to the man, 'See, I tell you this girl steal them,' and he say, 'It seems you right,' and then she ask me do I know the Bali custom if someone think to steal, and I say yes, and so she say it will be all right if I give her all the money I earn here at the hotel. I tell her again I never see that stuff before, but she say that unless I agree to give her all the money she will tell manager and I get fired."

"So you agreed, did you?"

"Yes, as soon as they pay me, I will give her the money." A puzzled frown furrowed Penebel's smooth brow. "I do not understand, *nyonya*. Myself I know I not take the jewels unless I do it in my sleep. And yet I know the gods will be very angry with this Negara and punish her very much if she make me pay for the stealing I have not made."

"There's an explanation for that," said Claudia. "But tell me, who is the man who came here with Negara that evening?"

"I not know, but he white man with light curly hair. He wear T-shirt with muscles so big they nearly split sleeves." A ghost of a smile hovered on Penebel's face.

"I happy to talk to someone here who believe me. Can you help me, *nyonya*? For myself the money not matter too much, but Tabanan and the Bedulu school, they need the money so much . . ."

"I'm certainly going to try," said Claudia, getting up from her chair. "Meantime, just try to forget the whole thing. Go on with your dancing, being as good as you possibly can, and if you get lonely, that nice boy downstairs would love to take you swimming."

She left Penebel then and made her way along the shadowy footpath to the main building of the hotel. She had made up her mind to confront Huntley Fox with the whole farcical story. If he believed Negara, he surely wouldn't condone her extortion of Penebel's salary, but he might fire Penebel. That was a risk Claudia had to take. With any luck Anton—for who else could the witness be?—might back up Claudia and say it seemed as though Negara knew the jewels were under the mattress all the time.

At any rate, she thought, anything was better than leaving the situation the way it was, with even Tabanan somewhat suspicious of Penebel, and Negara getting away with a rotten, spiteful act. Huntley must hear of this, and she, Claudia, was looking forward to telling him.

The first of the hotel guests to come down for dinner were filtering into the dining room as Claudia passed the entrance on her way up to the management floor. Huntley would still be there working away, she was sure. Her heart began to beat a little faster as she climbed the stairs.

She was heading for Eleanor Davis's glassed-in cubicle when she noticed a figure coming toward her —a tall feminine figure, slinking rather than walking, in spite of a bandaged foot. Negara!

Claudia hadn't prepared herself for bumping into

Negara before meeting with Huntley, but here was the villain herself, and there was no holding back the seething anger that welled up inside her at the moment of encounter. The two women stopped, facing each other a couple of feet apart, Negara wearing an expression of bored condescension, Claudia glaring like a cobra about to strike.

"Why, Claudia! I thought you'd left us. Or so I hoped."

"I came back because of you, you skunk!" Claudia spat back.

"What did you call me?" Negara's voice rose an octave.

Claudia glanced around. They couldn't argue out here in the open. Huntley was probably in his office and might hear them.

"Come in here." Claudia propelled Negara into the nearest office, which happened to be the assistant manager's. Shoving the dancer inside, she shut the door and stood with her back to it. Negara draped herself decoratively over the desk, one eyebrow quizzically raised.

"Would you kindly let me know what all this is about?" Negara's icy tone cut through the confined space of the room.

"I certainly will," Claudia came back. "Just tell me what prompted you to pull such a filthy trick on poor defenseless little Penebel?"

"Poor defenseless . . . The sneaky brat stole some of my best jewelry. She's lucky not to be in jail."

"She did not steal from you. You know perfectly well you rigged the whole thing simply out of spite because she's dancing instead of you. And dancing better than you ever could into the bargain. But she didn't quit. You underestimated her, didn't you? You never dreamed that she'd rather dance for nothing than not dance at all. She's a real artist—which is more than you are!"

"Don't be silly," said Negara with contempt. "It's obvious to everybody that she's just a little amateur. And rigging thefts isn't my line."

"You planted your jewels in her room. I know damn well you did!"

"How could I possibly have planted my jewels in her room? I didn't even know where her room was in that rabbit warren of a staff quarters."

"You could have found out easily. And then you went back there later when you knew she'd be there and pretended to find them under the mattress."

"Oh, so you know where she hid them, do you? You must have been talking to her, because nobody else knows. Lucky for her."

"What about your witness? Who was it, Anton?"

"Oh, yes, of course. Anton knows but he's sworn to secrecy to save the wretched little kid's name."

"But not to save her salary. You mean rat, extorting from her the promise to pay you everything she earns here!"

"Well," Negara shrugged, "she had to be punished somehow or other."

"You know you only did it that way to make Penebel either leave or suffer without your having to prove to anyone that she stole them. Because you knew that Huntley would never believe your story any more than I do. You took advantage of her Hindu faith, knowing she wouldn't fight back because of it."

"Huntley doesn't come into this at all," said Negara in a new firm tone.

"He does. And talking of theft, you set out deliberately to steal him from me and . . ." Claudia stopped herself. She hadn't meant these words to slip out.

"Steal Huntley from you? You stupid little fool, he was never yours in the first place. It was only when you started throwing yourself at him that I thought I'd better warn you off."

Claudia's hands were clenched hard by her sides. She felt her breath coming quicker. "I know he wasn't mine . . . yet. But in time he might have been. I loved him. I still do in fact, and I want him more than I've ever wanted any person or anything! But because you somehow have him mesmerized, I haven't a hope. And you don't love him at all. You could never make him really happy. You're only after him because Wilbur threw you over. You told me so yourself."

Scorn at Claudia's confession showed all over Negara's face. "It's entirely immaterial whether you love the man or I do. The only thing that counts is the fact that he's crazy about me, and not in the least interested in you."

"I know. That's why I left here a couple of days ago. It was just too painful to watch you manipulating the poor defenseless man. I . . . I couldn't bear it any longer."

"Another poor defenseless person for me to work on, eh? Yes, I enjoy my power over people, I must admit. I can control you too, can't I?"

"You cannot!"

"Well, when your presence in the hotel became intolerable to me, I got rid of you, didn't I? And that's just what I'm going to do again. Now that you've patted your precious little Penebel on the head, you can just put yourself into reverse and leave these premises pronto. Come on, off you go!" Negara got up from her chair, and started limping toward the door.

"I'm not leaving," said Claudia. "This business isn't finished yet. I'm going to see Huntley and tell him the whole story about you and Penebel and the jewelry."

"You think he'd believe you over me?" Negara laughed hollowly. "No, all he'd say is that if the girl was innocent, she naturally would have come straight to him about it instead of meekly handing over her salary to me to keep me quiet. In his eyes that in itself would prove her guilt."

"Never mind, I know what the truth is, and I think he should know too—or at least have the opportunity to make up his own mind. Honest, intelligent man that he is, he might just come down on Penebel's side in spite of the uncanny influence you have over him. I have a lot of trust in Huntley. I wouldn't love him if I didn't."

Negara laughed again, more mocking this time. "You're quite wrong, you know. I could tell Huntley the moon was made of green cheese and he'd believe me. He'd even believe this story about Penebel without question."

"So you admit it's a lie! You did plant that stuff in her room!"

"I didn't say that. But anyway it's no business of yours. Come on, get going! I have other things to do now." She advanced again.

"I won't!" shouted Claudia. "I'm going to Huntley right now!"

She flung open the door at the same moment as Negara let out a hiss and lunged toward her, grabbing at the sleeve of Claudia's dress with one hand and punching her with the other. "Oh, no, you don't!"

muttered the dancer as Claudia fled, narrowly missing a kick from Negara's shoe.

Limping on her bandaged foot, Negara chased Claudia through the door and across the clerks' office space. Suddenly Claudia ran straight into the arms of Huntley Fox.

CHAPTER TWELVE

Claudia screamed and clung to Huntley, her eyes flashing with anger as she looked back over her shoulder at Negara. The dancer had stopped dead in her tracks, her body suddenly slumped and her arms hanging limply at her sides. Her mouth drooped open stupidly; it was the only time Claudia had ever seen Negara out of control of a situation.

Huntley held Claudia to one side and reached out the other hand toward Negara. "You won't get what you want that way, Negara," he said in a soft voice.

She stared at him without a word, and then lowered her head, her long dark lashes shielding her eyes from Huntley's severe countenance.

"Come into my office, both of you," he commanded, jerking his head at Negara to lead the way. Claudia had largely recovered from her fright by now, but she was in no hurry to give up the reassuring support of Huntley's arm. Not until they were all in his office, where Negara was rapidly composing herself on the sofa, did he let Claudia go and indicate the easy chair she was to occupy. He himself went over to his desk and picked up the phone.

"Give me the house detective's room," he said into the mouthpiece, and a moment later, "Johnson? Manager here. I want you to go over to the staff quarters and pick up the young Balinese dancer who started with us last week. Her name is Penebel. There's a question of her having stolen something. Bring her up to my office right away. Oh, yes, and ask Mr. Reinholtz to come up too."

As he replaced the instrument on its cradle, Negara hunched one shoulder sensuously toward him, and said, "Darling, there's really no point in questioning that girl about the robbery. She'll only deny the whole thing, as I was trying to explain to Claudia here when you dropped by. And I really wanted you kept out of it; if you let her know you know about it, you'll have no alternative but to fire the poor child. That isn't really necessary as I've got my stuff back and . . . well, I'm quite prepared to forget the whole thing." She laughed, a slight titter, before adding, "And don't take my assault on young Claudia too seriously—it was just a joke, really."

While Negara had been talking, Claudia had been thinking. "Huntley," she said, "how did you know we had been talking about Penebel?" Who on earth, she wondered, could have told him about the country girl's alleged theft?

Huntley turned to Claudia and said in a rather worried tone, "You suddenly left us two days ago. Why?"

" I . . . I couldn't see myself studying Japanese grammar fifteen hours a day. You see, I came to Bali to learn about dancing, not a new language. I know I should have come to see you first, but . . . but I didn't dare to. I thought you'd be angry and I didn't want that."

He smiled, a slow cautious smile, but it made Claudia's heart jump. "I wouldn't have been angry; I think I would have understood. Anyway, I'm glad you came back tonight. When all this business is over, we can have a little chat."

"Darling," Negara was trying again, "do we really have to go through all this?"

"I'm afraid so," Huntley answered without looking at her.

She sighed loudly and tossed her head back. "Well then, darling, do you think I could at least have a drink to help it along."

"Not tonight, Negara," he said sharply. Then in answer to a knock on the door, "Come in."

Looking absolutely terrified, Penebel was ushered in by a portly man whom Claudia had seen around the hotel in shorts and a Hawaiian shirt; she had taken him for a guest, not the house detective. Behind them came Anton, his usually cheerful, well-balanced features marred by a frown of bewilderment and annoyance.

Huntley dismissed the detective and sat the other two down, completing the circle around the coffee table. Tension filled the air.

"Penebel," the manager began, "did anybody here in this room come and see you at the staff quarters two nights ago?"

Penebel nodded and tried to speak, but ended up pointing shyly at Negara and Anton.

"And what did they do there?" Huntley pressed her gently.

"They found some jewels under my mattress," Penebel replied in an almost inaudible voice, staring at her feet.

"And had you ever seen those jewels before?"

Penebel shook her head vigorously, "I . . . don't remember ever seeing them . . . but the lady tells me I stole them, so . . ."

"Go on, Penebel," he urged.

"So I must have done it in my sleep. But I honestly didn't know I had." She turned her large, misty eyes on Huntley. "Please believe me, sir. The lady has them back now, sir."

"And did you promise the lady to give her something she asked for, as is the Balinese custom when someone steals from someone else?"

"Yes, I did," said Penebel, earnestly contrite. "I will give her all the money I earn here at the hotel. I hope that is enough, sir, for me to be forgiven."

Huntley nodded slowly, and for a minute there was silence in the room. He turned to Anton. "Anton, do you agree with Penebel's story?"

The recreational director shifted uneasily in his chair. "Yes, I do. The mattress I was lifting when Negara found her jewels underneath."

"Was it your own idea to look under the mattress?"

"No . . . I think Negara suggested it."

Negara directed a bored smile at Huntley. "Not a very bright place to choose, was it? But then she's not a very bright girl."

Huntley took no notice of Negara's interjection, but continued to question Anton. "How did you come to be with Negara when she went to Penebel's room that evening?"

"She asked me to go with her. As a witness."

"I see. So she expected to find her missing jewelry there, did she? In fact she was so certain of it that she took you along as a witness to where she found it. Even though she didn't *know* it was there at all."

Negara butted in again. "It was pretty obvious, actually. I mean who else in this hotel would be so dazzled by some little semiprecious stones except a young country girl? And it's well-known that they're all terrible thieves up in the hills. Naturally I suspected her at once."

"Anton," said Huntley, "did Negara ask the way to Penebel's room when you arrived at the staff quarters?"

"No, she just led me straight upstairs and down all those corridors until we came to the right door. Why?"

Huntley turned to Negara for the first tmie. "How did you know your way to Penebel's room, Negara?"

"Somebody told me . . . beforehand. Yes, it was the first day she arrived at the hotel. I wanted to go and greet her and thank her for coming to fill in for me until my ankle got better—sort of a friendly gesture, you know. So I went over to the quarters and someone took me up to her room but she wasn't there. That's how I knew where she lived."

Huntley stood up. A deep sigh escaped from his chest. "All right, Anton, that's all for now, thank you. And you can go too, Penebel. I want you to forget all about those jewels. If you did take them, it was in your sleep, so you don't need to be punished for that. I'll see that you get to keep all your salary and that Tabanan gets an equal amount for his school as we arranged."

Penebel's expression changed miraculously to one of overwhelming joy. She leaped to her feet in a little dance, bending her knees as she landed. "Oh, thank you, sir!" she cried. "Now I am so happy! When you called me, I was just going to swim with my friend—now I will swim with much more happiness."

"Kardha certainly didn't waste any time following up, did he?" Claudia smiled. "I only introduced you to him an hour ago."

When Anton and Penebel had left, Huntley turned to Negara. Claudia stood uncomfortably in the background.

"I'm afraid I have all the evidence I need," he said. "There's no doubt in my mind that you planted your jewelry in Penebel's room and then accused her of stealing it. I can appreciate your motive too: spite. Or the hope that she would leave us. But at any rate it's something I can't tolerate in this hotel. So I'm going to have to let you go. It's a grave disappointment to me, I can tell you. But I insist that you catch the first flight to Jakarta tomorrow. The chief accountant will have a check for your pay until the end of the month. Good-bye, Negara."

Rage flared in her huge green eyes. "You think I'm going to take that lying down? You can't get away with it. Not with me."

"I'm firing you, Negara. And you have no Wilbur to turn to now."

"Yech!" The vulgar word sounded doubly coarse coming from such an exquisite mouth. "You and your damned morality! You'll never get anywhere in this world. I'm not wasting any more time on you."

She turned on her heel and stalked out of the room, slamming the door behind her.

Huntley stood staring at the closed door for a long minute; he took a clean white handkerchief from his breast pocket, shook it open, and dabbed his forehead. Elated though she was at the turn of events, Claudia couldn't help feeling a tinge of sorrow for him.

"That must have been very hard for you to do," she said quietly.

He pierced her with his searching eyes before

answering. Then the corners of his mouth crinkled into a wan smile as he said, "Not as hard as you might think. I certainly couldn't have done it two weeks ago—maybe not even one week ago. Thank you for making it easier for me, Claudia."

"Me?" she said. "How could I . . . oh, you mean by insisting that you hear about the Penebel affair?"

"I didn't mean that," he replied, but Claudia missed her chance to ask what he did mean, because an extraordinary thought had just struck her.

"Huntley . . ." she began hesitantly. "I don't understand. You seemed to already know the details of Negara's accusation of Penebel. Even who the witness was. I mean, all you could have heard when you came out of your office was me telling Negara that I was going to see you whether she liked it or not. You couldn't possibly have known what I was going to see you about."

"Oh, but I did know. I knew the whole story before you ever came in here."

"How? Nobody but Negara and Penebel and me and Anton knew. Did Anton tell you?"

"No, you did." His eyes were definitely twinkling now.

"I did? What do you mean?"

"The intercom between this room and the assistant manager's office happened to be switched on the whole time you were in there. So I could hear every word both of you said, including Negara's virtual confession of having planted the stuff at the end. That's when I thought I'd better intervene."

Claudia was so amazed at this news that she laid a hand on Huntley's arm for support while she absorbed it. He responded by slipping his arm around her waist.

"It's just as well I did. Negara in a fury is not as

dangerous as an Iban headhunter with a scimitar, but bad enough."

She looked up at him. "So you saved me from both."

"Fortunately."

She leaned her head against his chest without considering the intimacy of the gesture. She was still puzzled and going over in her mind the details of her conversation with Negara that he had overheard. "Tell me, Huntley, how did you know for sure that Penebel was innocent and Negara guilty of a frame-up?"

"Because she told you in the assistant manager's office that she couldn't have planted the jewels in Penebel's room because she didn't know which her room was 'in that rabbit warren,' as she described it. Yet she told me in here that she was able to lead Anton straight there because she had tried to visit Penebel the first day she arrived in the hotel. Her conflicting statements made a liar of her."

"I see. So you also heard her admit that she was only making a play for you now because she had lost out with Wilbur. That must have hurt."

"I suspected as much. And it didn't hurt nearly as much as it might have. Because of something else I heard over that dinky little machine. Something far more important."

"Oh," said Claudia. "What would that have been?" Then suddenly she knew. She pushed away from him and groped her way backward to the sofa, clutching its back with one hand, the other clamped over her mouth. He watched her in frank amusement. Gradually her hand dropped away and she was able to speak. "You . . . you heard me tell Negara that I . . . I . . . was in love with you! Oh, *Donnerwetter!*"

"I think that means 'thunderstorm,' doesn't it? You Germans have rather nice expletives." He held out his arms to her. "Come over here and let me show you that you've nothing to be ashamed of."

"You . . . you weren't meant to know," she whimpered. "That's the real reason I left, not what I told you. If I thought that you . . . you could ever, you know, feel the same way, I would learn Japanese and Chinese and anything you wanted." As she spoke, she inched her way across the carpet toward him, walking on cotton wool, her unblinking eyes glued to his smiling face. Then she reached him and he folded his long arms around her, lowering his mouth until it brushed against her own. Her hands moved upward into his hair, pulling his face against hers in an uncontrollable token of love. For several minutes they didn't move.

A heavy banging on the door broke them apart. Huntley answered the second thumping on the door with a brisk, "Come in."

Anton marched in, stiffly proud, leading Hilda, looking equally triumphant, by the hand. Both were beaming. For all the world they looked like the winning double in a tennis championship, coming forward to receive their trophy.

"Excuse please, Huntley," Anton said. "I have the great news. A telegram from Malibu office in San Francisco. I go to Kitzbühel in Austria as *Skidirektor*. Wilbur Fox, he arrange as he say he might."

Huntley nodded and smiled. "Ah . . ."

Anton turned to look cowlike at Hilda. "I think perhaps Hilda's father he talk to Wilbur last week. Hilda's father very important man."

"So . . . *wir fallen zusammen*," added Hilda, acknowledging her part in their common plans.

"She says Anton will be going back to Europe with the Steiners," Claudia translated for Huntley's benefit. "In a day or two."

"Ah . . ." said Huntley again. Although looking cordial enough, he didn't seem to be capable of concentrating on the imminent departure of his recreational director, or on the budding romance between him and one of the guests.

Claudia filled in for the manager. "Very nice for you, Anton. Congratulations. I'm glad that you and Hilda are, er, hitting it off so well . . ."

"It is you who introduce us," Anton chuckled. "*Danke schön.*"

"*Ja, danke schön,*" echoed Hilda before whispering something in Anton's ear that made him nod and fumble in the hip pocket of his tight white pants until he brought out a photograph. Still grinning, he handed it to Huntley, who blinked at it and swallowed twice. Claudia went over to look at the photograph over his shoulder. It was a clear snapshot of herself and the manager leaning over an ornamental wooden bridge, clasped together in a very unbusinesslike attitude, gazing into each other's eyes.

"Hilda, she give me the picture," said Anton. "I think very nice. On the notice board a copy I put. Rekans, the chef, he see it there, and he say to me that he know all the time about you two, while everybody else think it is Negara . . ."

"Well, they won't be thinking that anymore," said Huntley. "You'll be interested to know, Anton, that I just fired Negara. When she took you over to Penebel's room that evening, she knew all the time where the jewels were, as she put them there herself."

"So . . . o-o!" Anton whistled. "A good thing is it that my transfer to Kitzbühel comes before Uncle Wilbur hears about that which Negara did. He will be very angry, and maybe I lose my favor with him, *nein?* But now it not matter. My Hilda and I we go to Europe anyway." He put an arm like a steel band

around Hilda and squeezed. She looked at him ador-
ingly.

"Yes . . . well . . . that's very good," said Huntley,
flicking back his lock of hair. "Er, perhaps you'd run
along now, both of you. I'll see you before you go.
But I have something to discuss with Claudia . . ."

Hilda giggled, "*Ja, ja! Nach dem foto . . .*"

"*Komm, Herzchen!*" Anton wheeled her around and
they left the room, Hilda throwing a last giggle over
her shoulder at Huntley and Claudia, left standing
awkwardly, the incriminating photograph in front of
them.

"Well, it looks as though the cat's out of the bag
now," said Huntley. "By tomorrow the whole staff
will know I've sacked Negara and they will have seen
a copy of this picture. So you and I, Claudia, will be
romantically linked, as they say in the Sunday news-
papers."

"It looks like it . . ." replied Claudia nervously, her
heart beginning to pound at her nearness to him and
the way his gaze was penetrating her.

"For my part, I'd like to put the whole matter
straight. How about you?"

"Yes . . . yes," she croaked. "I agree."

"Well, then, there are two ways of doing that. One
would be for me to send you away too . . ."

Claudia's face drained of color and she felt suddenly faint.

"But a better way," he went on, "would be for me
to propose to you, because then the decision would be
in your hands."

"You mean . . . ?" she gasped, reaching for his
lapel.

"Yes, my love, that's just what I mean. Will you
marry me?"

"But, Huntley, I . . . I can't believe you really want me as your wife."

"I do, my darling," he smiled. "And as soon as possible."

"In that case . . . of course I will. You know I adore you." She buried her brimming eyes against the coolness of his shirt.

"I nearly died when I heard you'd run away," he said, stroking her hair. "I think I realized then how desperately I loved you. But I had sort of known it for a long time. The first stirrings came that evening when Anton brought you up here to get you a job. I had to think of some way to keep you in the hotel."

"But then," she said, raising her face again, "why didn't you just go along with his plan to hire me as a dancing teacher?"

"Because that way you'd have been reporting to him, and you'd have been seeing far too much of him for my liking. And not nearly enough of me."

"I see. To think that my whole fate depended on a group of important Germans arriving a few days later!"

"I'd have found something else for you to do, don't worry. In fact, when the Germans left, I had to. I didn't really need a hostess anymore since no other VIPs were due for a while, and the only thing I could think of was to suggest that you came to Borneo with me. That way I knew we could spend some time together so that perhaps you'd get to like me enough . . . enough to consider marrying me."

"Negara kept insisting that you wanted me to be seen around with you as a cover-up for the affair you were having with her. There were times when I felt sure she was right."

Claudia felt his body stiffen. Then his dark eyes

searched hers, questing. "I promise you, I never considered such a rotten trick. And I never had an affair with Negara. She fascinated me, I must admit, but not at all in the way I was interested in you. After all, even in those days, I had to dream up some excuse to get you to stay."

"You didn't, you know." She put up a finger to smooth the creases on his forehead. "I've loved you since before we went to Borneo."

His solemn look slid away. "And I was so jealous of Anton Reinholtz! Especially when you told me you were attracted to him . . ."

"That was nonsense," she cut in quickly. "I just invented it to hide my feelings for you."

"What a game this is, this game of love!"

"Isn't it?" She snuggled against him again, and then suddenly pushed away. "That reminds me. If you just wanted me here to be near you, why did you set me to trying to learn Japanese in a week? Fifteen hours a day indeed! That's no way to treat a girl you love."

"I made that up about a party of Japanese coming here. It was to give you something to do for this week, since I knew I was going to be too busy to spend much time with you. I didn't want you hanging around with a chance of meeting other men."

"What a nerve!" she exclaimed. "I was scared to death that I wouldn't be able to do it, and that you'd be mad with me. I . . . I couldn't bear the thought of that. It was one of the reasons I left."

"I'm sorry," he said contritely. "But you can just stay here as a guest now. I'll trust you now we're engaged, and I'll pay for your board and lodging until we get married."

"When's that going to be?" Claudia asked, her eyes glistening with anticipation.

"I'd suggest we wait until I'm sent back to San Francisco. I'm to be the new Vice-President for Administration for Malibu Hotels' head office."

"That's going to happen?" she said breathlessly. "Oh, I'm so glad. The only thing that was worrying me was the thought of being married to a man who works as hard as you do here."

"Yes, the directors feel that I've done my stint of managing. Wilbur told me the other day. He doesn't think I'm any good at it anyway."

"He just doesn't know!" said Claudia decisively, and then added rather sadly, "I hope we don't have to wait too long . . ."

"You'd rather be married in your hometown, wouldn't you, than out here?"

"I would really. With my family at the wedding and everything."

"Let's do that, then. Meanwhile . . ." He held her dainty hand between his large, gentle ones and their eyes locked again. "Meanwhile there will be plenty of time to show you just how much I love you." He drew Claudia into his comforting embrace and began kissing her deeply, tenderly. The multitude of problems related to the Bali Breezes Hotel were temporarily forgotten.